PRIZE SURPRISE
SWEEPSTAKES

OFFICIAL ENTRY COUPON

This entry must be received by: OCTOBER 30, 1995
This month's winner will be notified by: NOVEMBER 15, 1995

YES, I want to win the Sharp ViewCam! Please enter me in the drawing and let me know if I've won!

Name_____

Address _____ Apt. _____

City   State/Prov.   Zip/Postal Code

Account #_____

Return entry with invoice in reply envelope.

© 1995 HARLEQUIN ENTERPRISES LTD.   CVC KAL

PRIZE SURPRISE
SWEEPSTAKES

OFFICIAL ENTRY COUPON

This entry must be received by: OCTOBER 30, 1995
This month's winner will be notified by: NOVEMBER 15, 1995

YES, I want to win the Sharp ViewCam! Please enter me in the drawing and let me know if I've won!

Name_____

Address _____ Apt. _____

City   State/Prov.   Zip/Postal Code

Account #_____

Return entry with invoice in reply envelope.

© 1995 HARLEQUIN ENTERPRISES LTD.   CVC KAL

"Don't tell me you're divorced or you're a single parent?"

"I am neither, but then again I never told anyone that I was. Could we be at cross-purposes here?"

Davina frowned. "Does that mean to say," she said slowly, "that you have no living wife, or no wife living with you?"

Steve Warwick regarded her with enough scorn to wither most people, but Davina didn't even flinch as he said, "Let me try to set this straight in your mind, Mrs. Hastings. I am not married and therefore, as night follows day, I don't have a wife—do you think you're able to understand it now?"

"No mistress, de facto or whatever you like to call it?" Davina merely inquired, refusing to be deterred.

"No mistress, no live-in lover—no, *none* of those things. Why," he said in a voice loaded with mockery, "is it disturbing you to this extent, Mrs. Hastings? Please do explain."

LINDSAY ARMSTRONG was born in South Africa but now lives in Australia with her New Zealand-born husband and their five children. They have lived in nearly every state in Australia and tried their hand at some unusual—for them—occupations, such as farming and horse training—all grist to the mill for a writer. Lindsay started writing romances when their youngest child began school and she was left at a loose end. She's still doing it and loving it.

Books by Lindsay Armstrong

HARLEQUIN PRESENTS
1487—LEAVE LOVE ALONE
1569—DARK CAPTOR
1593—AN UNUSUAL AFFAIR
1656—UNWILLING MISTRESS
1693—A DIFFICULT MAN
1713—AN UNSUITABLE WIFE

Don't miss any of our special offers. Write to us at the following address for information on our newest releases.

Harlequin Reader Service
U.S.: 3010 Walden Ave., P.O. Box 1325, Buffalo, NY 14269
Canadian: P.O. Box 609, Fort Erie, Ont. L2A 5X3

LINDSAY ARMSTRONG

A Masterful Man

Harlequin Books

TORONTO • NEW YORK • LONDON
AMSTERDAM • PARIS • SYDNEY • HAMBURG
STOCKHOLM • ATHENS • TOKYO • MILAN
MADRID • WARSAW • BUDAPEST • AUCKLAND

ISBN 0-373-11770-1

A MASTERFUL MAN

First North American Publication 1995.

CHAPTER ONE

DAVINA HASTINGS breathed a sigh of relief and un-clenched her hands. She didn't feel at home in small planes and the one she was in that had just landed was very small indeed. An eight-seater, it had seemed extra-ordinarily fragile to her to be flying across three hundred miles of the South Pacific from the Australian mainland to the island of Lord Howe. Fragile and cramped, so that she'd had to battle with claustrophobia as well as her other fears. Then, to compound matters, they'd had to descend through a storm to the airstrip—that was when she'd closed her eyes.

But, as the little plane zipped towards the terminal, she looked eagerly out of her window to gain some impression of Lord Howe, reputedly a gem of an island and a photographer's paradise, only to see a mist-wreathed mountainside and driving rain.

'Sorry about this, folks,' the pilot said cheerfully. 'The weather, I mean, but I can tell you this is an isolated front on its way to New Zealand and it should be fine as soon as it passes through, and it should do that quite quickly. Thank you for flying with our airline and I hope you all have wonderful holidays!'

Davina grimaced. From their conversation it had been apparent she was the only passenger not coming to this paradise on holiday, and for a moment she ardently wished that were not so. But a job was a job, and she squared her shoulders and took herself in hand as she prepared to disembark.

The terminal was tiny, she saw, as she ran through the rain. Then she was through the glass doors, brushing raindrops from her hair and shaking them from her jacket and blouse and she looked up, straight into the eyes of a tall man lounging beside the counter. And it was not hard to read, as their gazes caught and clashed, that he was looking her over in the way men did when they were mentally undressing a woman, and, although in a curiously sardonic way, giving her the benefit of his unasked for approval.

Davina looked away from those rather hard grey eyes expressionlessly yet she found she was inwardly fuming and wondered why—it was not as if it had never happened to her before. In fact, it sometimes gave her cause for amusement, the fact that she had the kind of figure that attracted a lot of attention, darkish fair hair, darker eyebrows, and violet eyes set in a classically oval face. Amused her because her pin-up exterior didn't quite match her prosaic, practical, down-to-earth inner self and because if, as many men contrived to make her aware, she was the kind of girl they dreamt about, none of them had yet set *her* dreams alight.

But this is a bit different, she thought. For some reason or other, this man contrived to say that she might be good to bed but that would be the sum total of it—how dared he? Or did she imagine it?

She pondered for a moment longer, still determinedly looking the other way, then shrugged and decided she ought to make herself known to whoever had come to pick her up. But the little terminal was bustling and crowded now as resort employees gathered their guests and their luggage, the only staff member the airport boasted, apparently, was on the phone and no one appeared to be looking for a Davina Hastings, engaged as the temporary housekeeper for a Mr S. Warwick and his family.

So she collected her luggage and looked around again. The crowd was starting to thin and the tall man who had been leaning against the counter now had his back to her and his hands shoved irritably in his pockets as he scanned the retreating stream.

Then the pilot came in from the tarmac and, with a look of delighted recognition, came straight over to her. 'Hi!' he said. 'Thought I might have missed you. Where are you staying? I wondered if we could have dinner together, I'm staying overnight.'

Davina groaned inwardly as she thought, Another one! But this one, in his smart navy uniform, at least looked engagingly friendly as he held out his hand—he also looked to be about her own age, which was twenty-five, and he went on ingeniously, as they shook hands, 'It's D. Hastings, isn't it? I checked the passenger list and there was only one Hastings and you appeared to be the only one on your own, you're also not wearing a wedding-ring so I thought, in those circumstances, you might not mind my asking!'

Davina glanced involuntarily at her left hand and opened her mouth, but before she could speak a deep growling voice said, '*Hastings*?' And added with considerable biting annoyance, 'Oh, for crying out loud— don't tell me *you're* Mrs Hastings!'

Davina turned slowly, but she knew who it was. And as their gazes locked for a second time, she realised his eyes weren't entirely grey but had yellow flecks in them and that this man, whom she had a horrible feeling was Mr S. Warwick, was broad-shouldered as well as tall, was probably in his middle thirties and carried an aura of dynamism and, at this moment, angry power that struck out like a rapier. So that, despite wearing faded corduroy trousers and a bulky, nondescript sweater, despite having irregular features and windswept tawny hair and a tendency to freckles, you couldn't fail to be aware that he was very much a man of the world and very used to getting his way...

Davina blinked once, as she thought, so what? She said coolly, 'I am Mrs Hastings, yes. Who are you?'

He didn't answer immediately but he subjected her to a scathing reappraisal then said bitterly, 'I don't believe it! I *told* them I wanted a competent yet middle-aged, motherly sort of person, and what do they send me? Some aspiring film starlet who's probably just waiting for the right B-grade movie so she can take her clothes off!' he marvelled.

Two things happened simultaneously. Davina took a step forward with every intention of hitting him, and the pilot, who'd been looking almost comically confused, said hastily, 'I say, Mr Warwick, sir——'

'Get lost, Pete,' S. Warwick said briefly. And, to Davina's amazement, with a sheepish look, that was just what the pilot did.

'I don't believe this,' she said through her teeth. 'Who the hell *are* you? Anyone would think you own the island and have set yourself up as some kind of self-styled *pasha* able to make free with your insults and order people around as if they were dogs!'

S. Warwick raised an eyebrow. 'I do own a fair slice of the airline, so you'll have to forgive Pete for deserting you in your hour of need,' he drawled and added, 'Why *aren't* you wearing a wedding-ring, Mrs Hastings? Or did the agency mislead me about that as well?'

'They did not,' Davina replied cuttingly. 'I am a Mrs and whether I choose to wear a wedding-ring or not has nothing to do with you! I am also extremely competent at housekeeping and if someone needs mothering, I'm quite prepared to mother them——' She stopped abruptly and her eyes narrowed. 'But why *mothering*? Don't tell me you're divorced or you're a single parent?'

'I am neither, but then again I never told anyone that I was—could we be at cross purposes here?'

Davina frowned. 'Does that mean to say,' she said slowly, 'that you have no living wife, or no wife living with you?'

He regarded her with enough scorn to wither most people but Davina didn't even flinch as he said, 'Let me try to set this straight in your mind, Mrs Hastings. I am not married and therefore, as night follows day, I don't have a wife—do you think you're able to understand it now?'

'No mistress, *de facto* or whatever you like to call it?' Davina merely enquired, refusing to be deterred.

'No mistress, no live-in lover...no, *none* of those things. Why,' he said in a voice loaded with mockery, 'is it disturbing you to this extent, Mrs Hastings? Please, do explain.'

Davina set her teeth and said impatiently, 'Because if someone needs mothering it's got to be a motherless child...' She stopped and glared at him. 'Then I have to tell you I *never* work for single men, Mr Warwick,' she said. 'And I'll even tell you why! Single men, be they widowers or whatever, for reasons best known to themselves, tend to regard housekeepers as fair game—which you yourself proved as soon as you laid eyes on me. So what we have here now is not that the agency misrepresented me to you, but you to me.' She smiled, but not with her eyes; in fact they were as cold as ice. 'They actually told me you had a wife and daughter. I wonder why they would have done that, Mr Warwick, since you've made it so obvious it's not so?'

He was silent for a moment then a faint smile twisted his lips and he said smoothly, 'It had to be a misunderstanding, I'm afraid. What I have is a stepmother and a half-sister all bearing the name of Warwick. So that anyone checking the names in the household would have come across a Mr Warwick, a Mrs Warwick—there'll be two of those in fact, and a Miss Warwick aged eight. I would imagine *that's* how things got garbled, Mrs Hastings, wouldn't you agree? Moreover, the other Mrs Warwick is my grandmother—I wonder if you feel that array of woman-power on the scene is enough to keep you safe from the ravages of single men, Mrs Hastings? I'd be really interested to know.'

Davina stared at him and could have killed whoever it was at the agency who had 'garbled' things. Then she retorted, 'And *I'd* be really interested to know how you would hope to get away with presenting a housekeeper who resembles a B-grade film starlet to your stepmother, your half-sister and your grandmother!'

'Oh,' he grinned, 'they usually accept whatever I tell them to.'

Davina compressed her lips, and said with suppressed violence, 'Do you really believe I could work for you now? No, Mr Warwick, you may be able to walk all over your female relatives but it would be a grave mistake to think I was in that category. I'll go straight back.' And she turned away, as much because she was actually trembling with rage as with disgust.

'You can't,' S. Warwick said after a moment's thought.

'Can't *what*?' Davina queried, still turned away from him.

'Go straight back,' he said mildly.

That caused her to turn to him and say coldly, 'Of course I can go back—what do you mean?'

He observed her taut stance and the fact that the rain had caused her abundant hair to start to curl, then his gaze once more wandered over her figure, taking in things like the straight-cut beige linen jacket she wore over a now damp white silk blouse and slim white linen trousers, her beautiful narrow hands and the only ring she wore, a small gold signet on her little finger, her elegant flat beige leather shoes and her matching soft leather travelling shoulder-bag. Then his eyes rested briefly on her camera case before coming back to examine the smooth, faintly tanned skin exposed by the V of her blouse...

Which was when Davina said furiously, 'Now look here, Mr Warwick——'

'Of course you can *go* back,' he murmured then, looking amused. 'You just can't go *straight* back.'

'I...' Davina narrowed her eyes then glanced outside at the airfield. 'Are you telling me there are no more flights today?'

'Precisely,' he agreed.

Davina swore beneath her breath. 'Well, I presume there's somewhere I can put up for the night.'

'There is——'

'Other than with you,' she said pointedly.

He withdrew one powerful hand from his pocket and gestured amiably. 'There are actually four hundred beds on the island; I'm sure we could find you one. Or, it crossed my mind that you might be interested in...dispelling my first impressions of you, Mrs Hastings.'

'Dis... If you mean what I think you mean by that——' her eyes flashed '—I——'

'Proving to me that you're not a rather gorgeous, exotic creature who is totally unsuited to housekeeping is what I meant,' he said gravely. 'In other words, commencing your employment with me.'

'I thought I told you that was out of the question——'

'You did. But as *I'm* having second thoughts, why don't you?' And he looked at her with total, bland innocence.

Davina opened and shut her mouth several times before she was able to articulate her thoughts, a process S. Warwick watched with very polite attention. Finally, she said, 'Are you inviting me to believe that it would be possible for you to prove to *me* that you're not one of the most arrogant, unpleasant, insulting men I have ever met? A thorough bastard,' she said gently, 'to put it even more simply?'

He laughed and said one single word. 'Yes.'

'*No*——'

'Oh, come now, Mrs Hastings,' he said with a sudden rather weary and irritable lift of his shoulders. 'We got off on the wrong foot, can't we just leave it at that? Do you expect an apology—is that it? If so, I apologise——'

'Don't *bother*——'

But he overrode her in suddenly even, clipped tones. 'Look, if you must know, there would be few men immune from the sight of you running towards them in an open jacket and a white silk blouse that was getting wet.' A wicked little glint lit his eyes as Davina glanced down hastily and dragged her jacket closed. Then he continued drily, 'It's a fact of life I suspect, but I do apologise for my—momentary lapse in good manners or whatever the hell you like to call it. The other thing is, while I may have been a bit unfair in my remarks about B-grade movies, you just don't look like a housekeeper and I would take issue with *anyone* who tried to tell me otherwise!' He continued, with a returning flash of irritation, 'So. Yes, I admit I let myself vent my annoyance rather brutally on what I perceived as a muckup which is the last thing I can afford at present. You are not, however,' he said precisely, 'in any danger of being regarded as fair game in my household. I give you my word.'

'And why should I believe a thing you say?' Davina countered, but was struck by the odd little thought that she did... Why? she wondered. Because so ungracious an explanation and apology had absolutely nothing else going for it but the ring of truth? Perhaps...

And then, to make matters worse, S. Warwick said nothing more, nothing about there being any number of people who could testify to his word being his bond, just nothing. He simply stood there regarding her indifferently, but with that latent impatience and irritability not far away.

Davina tightened her mouth in exasperation and swung round with a toss of her head, only to stop still, arrested, as she stared through the glass doors that led to the car park on the other side of the terminal from the airfield. The rain had stopped and the sky partially cleared and her eyes widened and her lips parted as she looked her fill, then she turned back to the tall man and said huskily, 'Those mountains—what are they?'

'Mount Lidgbird and Mount Gower,' he said without a glance or a thought. 'Why?'

She swallowed. 'Would you mind if I photographed them? With that rainbow across them? Would there be a better vantage point?'

He frowned. 'Of course, but——'

'I don't think I've seen anything as spectacular and when I'm not moonlighting as a housekeeper I'm a passionate amateur photographer, you see. Mr Warwick,' she said with sudden decision, 'to be honest I doubt very much that you and I could work together in any sort of harmony, but I'm afraid I can't leave Lord Howe as soon as I'd planned—I need to photograph those mountains. So if we could postpone this discussion for a little while and if you could just direct me to a suitable spot before that rainbow fades, I'd be very grateful.'

Mount Gower and Mount Lidgbird, forming the southern end of Lord Howe Island, were not that high as mountains go, but what they lacked in height they made up for in many ways, Davina discovered, as she stood without her shoes on a wet grassy point opposite them. Dark, sheer and austere and rising straight out of the sea, with a threatening sky behind them and a rainbow shimmering across them, they quite took her breath away. White water boiled around their bases and all sorts of sea birds wheeled and called in a late afternoon frenzy about their craggy faces. And all this in the middle of this vast ocean, she thought, hundreds of miles from anywhere—I feel like Captain Cook! That's the only thing lacking: a tall ship threading its way through the reef...

And so absorbed was she, as she set up her tripod and started photographing, that it wasn't until with a sigh she took her last shot that she realised S. Warwick was standing a few paces away watching her thoughtfully.

'Oh. Thank you—the light's fading now so I won't take any more. I do appreciate your driving me here; you probably think I'm quite mad!' She telescoped her tripod and started to pack her camera away. 'Uh...' She looked around a bit blankly.

'You were going to say—what now?' he suggested with a trace of irony.

'Well.' She grimaced. 'Yes...'

'How about a drink?'

'Oh, I——'

'Don't argue, Mrs Hastings,' he returned. 'Just do as you're told. We still have a discussion to conclude—I think it's the least you owe me.'

Davina hesitated, but there was little she could do; there was no one about, no buildings that she could see, nothing but wild and wonderful Lord Howe and the South Pacific. So she climbed back into S. Warwick's unusually well-sprung Land Rover.

They didn't drive far, towards the base of Mount Lidgbird in fact and they did pass one guest-house before he turned off the narrow road on to a side track and they came to a small compound of houses in a valley.

'Is this it?' she enquired.

'This is it.'

'It's very—lonely,' she commented.

'It would take you about twenty minutes by bike to ride to the community hall, the so-called centre of the island,' he commented.

Davina said no more as she alighted and followed him through a stand of tall Norfolk pines towards the main house. And she had to admit that it was a lovely house built entirely of timber with two stories and a steeply pitched roof. She also noted that the front door was unlocked as she followed him through and she gasped with pleasure because, even in the fading daylight, she was presented with another marvellous view through wide glass windows of Mounts Lidgbird and Gower.

'Which is entirely why,' S. Warwick said, 'I chose this lonely spot.' And he waited a few moments before switching on some lights, thereby negating the view.

'I see,' Davina said a little lamely as she looked around and couldn't fail to be further impressed. From where they were standing, two steps led down to a large living-area and the wall of windows with their marvellous view, and it was all panelled in a deep, rich wood with shining wooden floors. Grouped at one end were three long, plump sofas around a large glass and forged-iron table. The sofas were covered in a shadowy chintz print in colours of pink and green and the forged iron was tinted an old, soft green that matched. In the other direction was a dining setting, again a glass and forged-iron table surrounded by eight chairs. There were a few occasional tables with lamps, and chairs scattered around, a beautiful Chinese carpet between the two settings and the whole impression was one of space, elegance and comfort.

She looked up and saw a soaring ceiling with a gallery running round it and guessed the bedrooms, or some of them, led off it, and she was just looking around for a staircase when he said, 'Sit down, Mrs Hastings. What would you like to drink?'

Davina hesitated again, which he took note of and said witheringly, 'I don't plan to make you drunk for the purposes of seduction in this lonely spot, believe me.'

She bit her lip and shrugged. 'All right. I'll have a brandy and soda, thank you. But——'

'But you don't entirely trust me yet,' he filled in for her with a certain malicious humour.

Davina cast him a speaking look and walked calmly down the two steps towards the sofas. But she did say over her shoulder, 'No, I don't. As to whether I could ever like you, I have the gravest possible doubts about that, too, Mr Warwick.'

'Well, I wouldn't worry too much about it,' he replied as he opened a tall, beautiful antique oak cabinet and pulled forward two glasses. 'You wouldn't be alone and we need see very little of each other.'

Davina tossed her head and sat down facing the view and presently he handed her a glass and sat down opposite her.

'Cheers,' he said. 'Would you care to tell me what you meant about being a photographer when you weren't *moonlighting* as a housekeeper?'

Davina sipped her drink then said wryly, 'An unfortunate choice of words. What I meant was that photography is . . . what I would like to be my chosen career, but it's not a career I make much money from, yet, so from time to time I do the other thing I'm good at which is temporary housekeeping. It's an ideal combination,

actually, and——' she paused and looked levelly at him
'—should you still be worried about that term *moonlighting*, I've been thoroughly vetted by the agency—
they have very high standards and they've checked me
out from top to bottom, so you can rest assured I won't
be pinching the silver or anything like that. I also have
a degree from a technical college in catering—does that
help you, Mr Warwick?'

He lay back and looked at her meditatively. 'So, you've
decided to do the job,' he said idly, at last.

Davina shot him a cold little look. 'No, I haven't, not
yet. I was merely trying to make the point that I'm trust-
worthy and respectable.'

'It still seems to be an odd combination,' he mused,
unperturbed. 'It also——' he looked down at his glass
and frowned '—indicates a preference for a gypsy sort
of lifestyle—how come?'

'Just the way I am, I guess,' she said blandly.

He raised an eyebrow. 'And then there's the jump from
catering college to photography.'

She said nothing but sipped her drink again.

'And how come,' he pursued, 'if you're so determinedly a "Mrs" you don't wear a wedding-ring?'

'I thought I told you, that's my business——'

'Well, not really.' S. Warwick sat forward. 'I mean,
were you—moonlighting as a married woman, for
example, for reasons best known to yourself,' he said
with soft satire and smiled a sort of tigerish little smile,
'it could be my business too.'

'I fail to see why.'

'I'll tell you—because if you were misrepresenting
yourself in one thing, you could do so in others, despite
being vetted from top to bottom.'

Davina grimaced. 'I still fail to see in what way it could affect this job. As a matter of fact, were I moonlighting in this respect, it would probably be to protect myself from——'

'All those ubiquitous single men that abound in the land? Ah! Is that the case, then?'

Davina stared at him with her nostrils flared. 'Unfortunately, no,' she said tautly and reached for her bag, then her purse from which she pulled a small gold object and slid it on to her left hand. 'There,' she said. 'My legitimate wedding-ring, and if you're right about one thing, Mr Warwick, the only misrepresentation involved is that I'm no longer married. But I believe I'm perfectly entitled to claim to be a Mrs, despite that small fact, and if you must know,' she went on in a goaded sort of voice, 'I do use the ring and the title when I'm on these kinds of jobs just in case I need the protection of them.'

'But you don't normally wear the ring.'

'How do you know?'

He shrugged. 'I noticed that the tan on that hand was unbroken. Did you forget to put it on?'

'Yes. Will you please drop the subject!'

'Why?' he said lazily. 'Surely you can tell me if he's dead or alive or has merely divorced you?'

'All right, we're divorced.'

'Why?'

Davina stared down at her wedding-ring, her expression frozen then she raised her remarkable violet eyes and was not to know how bitter and sombre they were as she said, 'If you really want to know, he thought I was a frigid bitch—among other things.' She sat forward and put her unfinished drink on the table. 'I'll go now.

I would hate to impose on you any further, so if you could call me a taxi, I'd be grateful.'

S. Warwick considered her for a moment before he said, 'Unfortunately, Mrs Hastings, I am unable to do that.'

'Why not? Look here.' Davina's voice rose a little shakily. 'I——'

'Only because there are no taxis on the island,' he said.

CHAPTER TWO

'OH FOR heaven's sake!'

Davina rose and stared at him with acute frustration.

He shrugged and looked amused. 'It's a very small island, Mrs Hastings. Barely seven miles long and two miles wide and most of it is uninhabited. The permanent population is roughly three hundred souls and there are six hundred bicycles—the much preferred form of transport for the, as I mentioned before, four hundred tourists the place can handle. I myself have four bicycles——'

'Well if you're about to lend me a bicycle I must decline,' Davina said tartly. 'You——'

'You've never ridden a bike?'

'Of course I have! I simply do not propose to do so now, in the dark, with my luggage.'

'That wasn't what I had in mind.'

She stared at him, breathing noticeably. 'Then why did you bring it up?'

He grimaced. 'I thought it might add some charm to the place. You obviously don't know a lot about Lord Howe, Mrs Hastings.'

'I don't,' she conceded ungraciously. 'I was, in fact, a last-minute replacement for the competent, motherly person they'd found for you—she broke her ankle. So I didn't have a lot of time to add to my rather vague knowledge of Lord Howe, but they did assure me it was extremely beautiful and a——' she hesitated '—photographer's paradise,' she finished on a suddenly weary downbeat.

S. Warwick smiled faintly but said nothing.

Davina looked around, clenched her teeth then sat down again. 'All right! Tell me more about the job—not that I've decided to do it,' she warned, 'but...' She gestured and shook her head exasperatedly.

He sat forward again. 'My... female relatives are due to descend on me shortly. They generally spend a holiday on the island at least twice a year. They also generally avoid each other like the plague but are coming together this time, I believe, in a bid to put family relationships on a better footing. If you had any idea what a horrifying prospect that is, Mrs Hastings, I'm sure you would take pity on me.'

Davina blinked. 'I don't understand—and I thought—forgive me,' she said ironically, 'but I got the distinct impression that one word from you and they behaved like perfect lambs.'

'That's not quite true, although they certainly do what I tell them to do—eventually. However, there's one area where even I have trouble controlling them and that is who has sovereignty over the ordering of the household.'

Davina, despite herself, found herself smiling a wry little smile. 'I see.' But she added, less amusedly, 'So, you're proposing to throw *me* into this lionesses' den of dispute?'

'Exactly,' he said without a shadow of remorse, then shrugged. 'Well, what I propose is to make it plain beyond any doubt that you're running the house.'

Davina thought for a moment. 'Why do they dislike each other?'

'Ah.' He drank some brandy. 'That's quite a long story,' he said drily, and looked at her as if he was in two minds.

Davina raised an eyebrow. 'It would be better if I knew—were I to take the job, Mr Warwick, and may I remind you that you showed no spirit of polite reticence at all concerning me, so I don't see why I should be at all polite to you.'

He chewed his lip then laughed softly. 'OK. After my mother died, my father remarried a woman young enough to be his daughter who bore *him* a daughter posthumously, thereby providing me with a half-sister young enough to be—my daughter. All of which induced a spirit, talking of those things, of fierce resentment and dislike in my grandmother—my father was her only child. She perceived that Loretta, my step-mother, married my father for his money, then spent a considerable amount of it, turned his life upside down and wore him into an early grave. Added to this, my grandmother is an indomitable, energetic and fiercely opinionated lady, anyway... Well, need I say any more?'

'No,' Davina mused, and frowned. 'Why does the child need mothering?'

'Because her mother is not much of a mother,' S. Warwick said, and there was something in his voice that was as cold as naked steel.

Davina narrowed her eyes but said only, 'A month...is not a long time for anyone else to do much mothering.'

'What I had more in mind was someone who is good with kids, someone who wouldn't mind babysitting without making the kid feel she's being—palmed off.'

'Well, that is being pretty frank, Mr Warwick,' Davina murmured.

'You asked for it, Mrs Hastings,' he replied.

'So I did.' Davina stood up again and looked around consideringly.

'If you're wondering how you would cope with this house and a child, I have a cleaning lady, a local, who comes several times a week—she's due tomorrow—and does the laundry as well,' S. Warwick said. 'To be honest she's a bit rough and ready and she's dynamite when it comes to breaking crystal and china, so while you can leave all the heavy jobs to her you will still need to—well, supervise, anyway. But all meals, as well as the entertaining we will undoubtedly be doing, would be up to you. What kind of things do you like photographing—only scenery?'

Davina turned slowly to look at him. 'No. Flowers, birds——'

'Ah.' He stared at her with the utmost gravity, something she was later to come to mistrust devoutly. 'Are you aware then, Mrs Hastings, that one third of the plants on Lord Howe are unique? That hundreds of thousands of sea birds nest here each year, and that one of the world's rarest land birds lives here? I won't bore you with all the species but the island is a haven for terns of all descriptions from Sooties to Noddies; red-tailed Tropicbirds nest here as well as masked boobies and Providence petrel, fleshfooted shearwaters, otherwise known as Mutton Birds, which nest in burrows in the ground... As for the plants, flowers and trees, there's pandanus, banyan, island cedar, island apple, juniper, sallywood, kentia—of course kentia palms——'

'As a blackmailer, Mr Warwick,' Davina broke in tightly, 'you're incredibly obvious.'

He said nothing for a moment then he murmured, 'You see me quite dashed, Mrs Hastings—by the way, did I mention that Lord Howe has the southernmost coral reef in the world?'

They eyed each other until he added, 'Besides which, we have Ball's Pyramid only a dozen or so miles south of the island—now that is certainly worth photographing.'

'What on earth...?' Davina bit her lip.

'Is Ball's Pyramid? A sheer, pointed, eroded stack of rock that is the world's tallest monolith and it floats out of the ocean like a castle in a fairy-tale.'

'Does one have to be a fairy to get to it?'

He grinned. 'Not at all; one takes a boat or you can fly over it. I happen to have a couple of boats,' he added modestly.

'Boats, bikes, airlines,' Davina muttered and sat down suddenly. 'I gather your troublesome female relatives have not yet arrived?'

'No. You have three days of—relative peace.'

'Why did you get me here so early?' she queried.

'Well now, seeing as I was expecting a competent motherly middle-aged type, you can't really accuse me of any nefarious intentions, can you, Mrs Hastings?' His eyes mocked her.

'Then *why*?' Davina said angrily.

'Simply so you would have a chance to acclimatise before you were expected to deal with them.'

She picked up her drink and sipped it distractedly.

'You have your own quarters, incidentally,' he said after a time. 'Would you like me to show you them before you make your final decision?'

*　*　*

One of the buildings behind the house was a chalet-type edifice which turned out to be a small but luxurious self-contained unit. There was a bedroom with a double bed, furnished in toning shades of smoky blue, a matching blue bathroom and a combined kitchenette and living-area with cane furniture, terracotta tiles on the floor, ivory blinds and soft sage-green walls. Everything, from the Sheridan bed-linen to the bathroom fittings, the quality of paint, enamel and tiling work, the co-ordination of colours was of an exceptionally high quality and standard. There was even a wall-phone.

Davina looked around with raised eyebrows.

'You're impressed, Mrs Hastings?' S. Warwick remarked.

'Very nice,' she contrived to say equitably. 'Very *House & Garden*, in fact.'

'Is that a compliment or the opposite?' he enquired.

Davina shrugged her slim shoulders. 'Just a bit of a surprise, perhaps. It looks more like a guest-house than staff quarters.'

'It doubles as either.'

'Well...' She didn't go on.

'I await your decision with bated breath, Mrs Hastings,' he said with irony after several moments.

They faced each other across the living-area and Davina discovered two things. That she would like nothing more than to tell him to go to hell, but that she couldn't quite bring herself to do it.

'Tell me something,' she said a little huskily as this dawned on her. 'What happens if I do turn out to be—exotic but quite useless?'

He smiled, just a bare twisting of his lips, his eyes remained a cool, watchful, curiously mocking hazel, and he said, 'I would pack you back to the mainland very swiftly, Mrs Hastings—but you aren't, are you?'

Davina licked her lips because she sensed an odd sort of tension between them that she couldn't quite define. 'How can you know, though?'

'I'll just have to rely on my intuition. In fact,' he said drily, 'I wouldn't be at all surprised if you were extremely competent——'

'That's a change of heart!' She flashed him a cutting little look.

'And intelligent,' he went on, unperturbed, 'and that is quite a waste, doing what you're doing with your life. I'd also be very surprised if you were a—frigid bitch, Mrs Hastings, but if you care to continue to masquerade as one, so long as it gets my job done, you're welcome to it.'

Davina gasped then paled slightly as she suddenly realised that this powerful, worldly man who could switch from insulting her with lazy mockery to malice aforethought *incensed* her, yet his attitude puzzled her... Why? she wondered numbly. I would have hated him if he'd made the traditional pass; I have to hate him as it is for... everything else; why should it be at all important to prove to him that I'm... anything?

'Mrs Hastings?' S. Warwick said, and added with sudden impatience, 'Look, if you really don't want the job, I'll send you back first thing tomorrow morning and they'll just have to find a replacement. It's up to you,' he added curtly. 'We've been——' he glanced at his watch '—fencing with each other for over an hour now and I'm getting tired of it. Yes or no?'

The effect of this was to wipe away all other thoughts from Davina's mind other than that he was the most arrogant bastard... 'Yes,' she said crisply. 'I'll stay.' And might just as well have said, So do your damnedest...

He raised his eyes ceilingwards. 'I might have known!'

'And what might you have known, Mr Warwick?' she asked through her teeth.

'That all the foregoing was entirely unnecessary. Women,' he said scathingly, 'have to be the most entirely unstraightforward creatures—God alone knows why!'

Davina held on to her temper by the narrowest margin. 'Oh, I suspect,' she said sweetly, although her eyes were an icy violet, 'that it's what we have to put up with from men that does it. I mean to say, in the space of a couple of hours I've gone from being suspected of wanting to take my clothes off at the first opportunity to——'

He laughed. All of a sudden he relaxed, the tension went out of his broad shoulders and the furious impatience drained from his expression. 'I excelled myself there, I'm afraid,' he said wryly.

She could have hit him; she was visited by the most intense anger she'd ever experienced and to make matters worse that keen hazel gaze missed none of it—and Davina passed suddenly from rage to fear. I must be mad, she thought. This man... is dangerous. He incites altogether too much emotion in me even if it is rage and hatred. I should have said no...

'You still can, Mrs Hastings,' he murmured, and her eyes widened.

'D-do what?' she asked unsteadily, hoping and praying that he hadn't read her mind.

'Tell me to go to hell,' he said softly. 'In fact, I'm wondering why you didn't. Care to enlighten me?'

'Yes.' She attempted to pull herself together. 'I think I was hoping to prove something to you——'

'Well, that's fine with me,' he broke in, 'so long as it isn't…anything to do with the taking off of your clothes.'

'Do you know,' she managed to say almost thoughtfully, she wasn't sure how, 'your preoccupation with that subject leads me to wonder about you, but you will really just have to accept my guarantee on the subject; I can say no more.' And she kept her gaze supremely steady as it rested on him.

'OK.' He shrugged. 'I guess if I expect you to take me on trust, I shouldn't mind doing the same.' He smiled suddenly and it was quite a devastating smile, full of life and wry humour, and with a further shaft of fear Davina realised that S. Warwick could be a devastatingly attractive man when he chose. 'Unfortunately,' he added, 'I have to go out, I have a meeting, but that might give you the opportunity to potter around by yourself and get to know the place—you have *carte blanche* and there's plenty of food in the kitchen to make yourself a meal. By the way, don't feel nervous; there's no crime on the island.'

'I notice you don't even lock your front door,' Davina said involuntarily.

'No. You can lock yourself in here, though, if you're so minded.'

Davina said nothing, although she still returned his gaze steadily.

'Well,' he murmured after a moment, 'goodnight, Mrs Hastings.'

'Goodnight, Mr Warwick.'

He turned to go but turned back. 'What does the D stand for?'

'Davina,' she said coolly.

'May I call you that?'

'You can call me what you like.'

'I see,' he said softly. 'I gather it would be no good offering to return the compliment?' He raised a lazy eyebrow at her.

'I don't know what you mean.'

'I mean I'm quite sure were I to ask you to call me Steve, that you would persist in addressing me as "Mr Warwick" with all the hauteur you're capable of.'

'You would be *quite* right, Mr Warwick.'

'I thought so. Goodnight, Davina. Sleep well.' And this time he left, closing the door gently behind him.

Davina took a deep breath then picked up a small cushion from the chair beside her and hurled it quite uselessly at the door.

Half an hour later she'd unpacked and was inspecting the main house. There were four bedrooms upstairs, all unusual, interestingly shaped rooms with steep ceilings and window-seats but three of them lacked any linen on the beds or in the *en suite* bathrooms. Steve Warwick's, which she looked into briefly, was done out in masculine fittings and the colour scheme was cream and green.

Downstairs she discovered that the gleaming kitchen was a cook's dream, with every kind of appliance one could wish for, all looking unused. There was also a breakfast-room-cum-sitting-room, a study that was entirely businesslike and contained a VHF radio, and a den with a television set. The laundry, which held a huge freezer, a shower cubicle and a linen store, was in an

annexe—together with the four bicycles. She surveyed
them for a long moment, then went back to the kitchen
where she made herself a simple meal of scrambled eggs
on toast.

Not long afterwards she took herself to bed and, despite the eerie quality of an almost silent night with just
one strange bird calling mournfully, fell asleep quickly.

'Ah, Davina, you're up bright and early.'

Davina looked up from the breakfast she was making
to see her employer lounging in the kitchen doorway.
He had on khaki shorts, a white T-shirt, his hair was
damp and tousled and his feet bare. She also wore a pair
of long khaki shorts, a neat pink blouse tucked into them
with a narrow leather belt around her trim waist and
polished leather moccasins. She'd tucked her hair behind
her ears and had only put moisturiser on her face and
a touch of soft coral lipstick. The effect, nevertheless,
because her thick hair shone and was well-cut, her skin
smooth and fresh, her nails perfectly manicured, was
one of good grooming and an air of purpose.

Steve Warwick took this all in as she merely nodded
at him and told him that she'd taken the liberty of
making him bacon and eggs this first morning.

He glanced at the pan she was tending. 'Bacon and
eggs suit me fine.' He strolled into the kitchen and pulled
a chair out from the table which was laid for one and
had a pitcher of freshly squeezed orange juice on it. 'It
seems to me that you've settled in rather well,' he
remarked.

'Well, there are one or two things we'll have to discuss,'
she murmured, and put a plate in front of him con-

taining not only bacon and eggs but fried tomato and banana. 'Uh—do you like coffee or tea for breakfast?'

'Coffee, thank you,' he replied politely.

Davina set the percolator on the stove and put fresh toast in a rack on the table. 'What about you?' he added.

'I've had breakfast, thank you.'

A gleam of amusement lit his eyes. 'Won't you at least join me for a cup of coffee? We could discuss whatever it is we need to discuss at the same time.'

'All right.' But she waited until he'd finished and cleared his plate away as the coffee bubbled gently and filled the kitchen with its delicious aroma. She poured two cups and sat down opposite him, hesitated, then decided to plunge right in. 'I've found that it's usually helpful to everyone to have a timetable for meals and, if there need to be any variations, if you'd let me know the evening before, I can make the necessary adjustments. I don't——' she paused and smiled faintly '—mean that to sound as if I'm some sort of martinet who'll be making everyone's life a misery if they're two minutes late for dinner.'

Steve Warwick wiped his long fingers on a gingham napkin. 'Not at all,' he drawled. 'I think it's an admirable suggestion. Go on.'

Davina warned herself against being entirely fooled by this compliance. 'But breakfast is a bit different when you're on holiday,' she continued, 'so——'

'Loretta and my grandmother only eat fruit and toast for breakfast. They can help themselves to that whenever they like. Candice and I usually eat breakfast together at around about this time. Otherwise make it twelve-thirty for lunch and seven for dinner.'

'Good,' Davina murmured after a moment. 'I see the bedrooms aren't made up—will Candice and her mother share or——'

'No.'

'OK. I'll fix them up the day before they arrive. What about food in general—any preferences? And would you like three-course dinners, for example, hot lunches? Does Candice join you for dinner?'

He shrugged. 'Yes, she does unless it's a dinner party and on those occasions three courses would be in order. Lunch you can make quite simple, cold meat and salad, that kind of thing—I leave it up to you.'

'So only two courses when you aren't entertaining?'

'Uh huh. We also catch and eat a lot of fish—are you good at cooking fish, Davina?' He raised an eyebrow at her.

'How nice for you—extremely good,' she said mildly. 'I noticed a barbecue outside—would it be in order to light it on the odd fine night? I'm even good at barbecuing fish.'

'Perfectly in order—is that the lot?' he said gravely, and Davina took a breath and set her teeth because it was back again. As he himself had put it, they were— albeit with the utmost politeness—fencing with each other once more.

And for the life of her she couldn't help herself as she said innocently, 'I think so. Are you about to rush off somewhere? Please don't let me detain you if so.'

'I'm about to take you on a tour of the island,' he replied equally as innocently.

She stood up, 'There's really no need for that, Mr Warwick. I found the bicycles so I can take myself, besides which, I ought to get to know your cleaning lady——'

'You can do that later, Davina. It so happens that this is the only free time I have at the moment.'

'But——'

'And I am quite determined to show you round the island, to introduce you to the local shopkeepers where you may shop for food or whatever you need on *my* account—there's also another Land Rover in the garage you can use—and to indicate to you the places you could visit with Candice so that you wouldn't be stumbling around in the dark, so to speak.'

Davina bit her lip as their gazes held and she perceived the bright irony in his. She sighed inwardly and reflected that the resolution she'd made on waking this morning, to do with somehow terminating all such exchanges between them, had failed. 'I'm sorry,' she said quietly. 'I'm ready whenever you are.'

He narrowed his hazel eyes but, and she couldn't believe it was to allow her to save face, said no more than, 'Give me ten minutes.'

Mounts Lidgbird and Gower presented quite a different image as they drove off. The sun sparkled on them, a few white clouds floated around their peaks, and Davina caught her breath.

Steve Warwick glanced at her with a lifted eyebrow.

'They just—get to me,' she said. 'Can you climb them?'

'Gower yes, but with a guide. Lidgbird is virtually inaccessible beyond the Goat House which is a bit over halfway up and so-called because it's a cave where the few wild goats left on the island shelter.'

'Are they indigenous?'

'No. They were put on the island to provide meat for any callers. Because of the damage they caused to the local flora they were then marked down for eradication.' He changed gear and turned on to the road over a cattle-grid.

'It's an incredibly beautiful island,' Davina said as they turned away from the mountains and she could see the lagoon with its turquoise water that hugged the western side of Lord Howe. 'Has your family always lived here? I'm afraid I don't know any of the history of the place.'

'Ah.' He grinned. 'Well, very briefly, it was discovered in 1788 by Lieutenant Lidgbird Ball when he sailed past on his way from Sydney Cove to Norfolk Island which became a penal colony. But until 1834 no one lived here although there were frequent visits from whaling ships and ships *en route* to Norfolk. The first settlers existed by trading provisions with passing ships and then in the late 1800s the Kentia palm, which is indigenous here, came wildly into vogue in European drawing-rooms and a flourishing trade in the sale of seeds became the island's main income—it still is today, together with tourism.'

Davina sighed and smiled. 'It's amazing, isn't it? I mean these islands of the South Pacific, Norfolk and Pitcairn, Norfolk with its awful history as a penal colony and both of them with their descendants of Fletcher Christian—and Lord Howe. It's a romantic part of the world.'

He grimaced. 'Are you a romantic, Davina?'

'In that respect, I guess I am,' she replied after a moment.

'Well, this is the airport, as you no doubt remember, and across the road here, up that incline and down the other side is Blinky Beach. If you're a good surfer it's great, but there are more protected beaches for kids.'

An hour later Davina had seen all there was to see by road of the island and had indeed been charmed. She loved the fact that there were no high-rise buildings, very few shops, an almost total lack of commercialisation and that most of the guest-houses and private dwellings were screened from sight behind luxurious, tangled foliage and the beautiful, tall, sometimes unbelievably tall, Norfolk pines. She loved the lush paddocks studded with yellow daisies and white clover and the lovely, secluded little beaches. She was introduced to the Kentia palm and saw her first white tern as they drove down Lagoon Road between towering walls of trees, and was amazed to be told that they laid their eggs on a bare branch, no nest, no nothing.

She was beguiled by the tiny community hall and the radio station alongside the only jetty the island boasted and she itched to don a back-pack loaded with her camera and explore the walking trails to places with be-witching names such as the Clear Place, Malabar, Mount Eliza. And everywhere on Lord Howe, she discovered, there were birds, from the island's distinctive landbirds like the plump, busy as a housewife emerald ground-dove, the Golden Whistler and the pied currawong to all the migratory species Steve Warwick had told her about—birds that performed unbelievable feats, to her mind, such as returning each year to the Arctic Circle or the North Pacific.

Another thing he'd been right about was the bicycles, and not only that, but the bicycle racks that were placed at every entrance and at the start of all the mountain trails and walks.

'It's amazing,' she said with a laugh as they inched past yet another group of cyclists all wearing crash helmets—the speed limit she'd noticed was twenty-five kilometres. 'And everyone wears a helmet!'

'Oh, our local policeman is very strict about that!'

'How is the island governed?' she asked curiously.

'Well, it's part of New South Wales but we have a local island board and an administrator who lives here. Since the island was inscribed on the World Heritage List, everyone's main aim has been to keep it as undisturbed as possible so that everything unique about it can flourish. That's why the tourist ceiling is set at four hundred, why there are no giant complexes and casinos et cetera. There are also no freehold titles on the island.'

Davina looked surprised.

'A rather sore point with some,' he said wryly.

'So you don't own your land?'

'Not freehold, no. We have a system of perpetual and special leases for islanders only, which is designed to protect the island as well as the locals. For example, if you wish to sell your lease it has to be valued and offered to island residents first, at that valuation. Only if it's not purchased by a resident may it then be offered for sale on the open market.'

'I suppose, then,' she said slowly, 'a lot of it is passed down from generation to generation.'

'You suppose right.'

'So—I asked you this before but we got sidetracked——'

'Yes, my grandfather was descended from one of the early families to settle on the island.'

Davina was silent for a time. It was obvious that Steve Warwick was a very well-respected resident of Lord Howe Island—everyone they'd spoken to had made that quite clear—and that he had a finger in a lot of pies. He'd shown her his two tourist boats that made sightseeing trips round the island, and fishing trips to Ball's Pyramid. He also owned a shop, a restaurant and a guesthouse. She glanced sideways at him involuntarily and found herself wondering why he'd never married. Because, if you were anyone else but her, you would have to admit he had an awful lot going for him. There was so much inherent ease and lightly held authority in his dealings with all the people they'd met, you could be forgiven for imagining him being—well, anything, she mused. There had been, only yesterday, evidence of how dangerous it was to cross him. There was the cultured way he spoke and his lovely house. And there was that unmistakable assurance of a man who was exciting to women...

'You were thinking, Mrs Hastings?'

Davina twitched her gaze away and felt her nerves prickle once more. You couldn't call the confines of the Land Rover cramped but it was impossible not to be aware of things like his hands on the wheel, the width of his shoulders, the length and strength of his legs, not to mention a rather powerful intelligence from which it was a little difficult to hide... She decided not even to try. 'I was wondering why you'd never married, Mr Warwick,' she murmured.

He lifted a wry eyebrow. 'What brought that on?'

Davina waved a hand. 'You seem to have a small empire here; you seem,' she paused, then went on deliberately, 'to have a lot of things going for you.'

'Are you saying that from the conviction that I should at least share it with a woman?'

'No. I don't hold those kind of convictions,' she replied calmly. 'But it is the accepted convention, if you like, for very normal reasons, and more so here than otherwise, I would imagine—keep the island in the family kind of thing.'

He grimaced, but said, 'Well, the answer is quite simple. I've never met a woman I—couldn't live without.'

'Dear me.' Davina had to smile. 'Are your standards impossibly high?'

He shot her a narrow, glinting little look. 'Perhaps.'

'Or are there times when you're just so—abrasive that no woman has been able to put up with you?'

'That could be true, too,' he agreed blandly.

'Well, you have got a problem, Mr Warwick.'

'Davina,' he said gently, 'don't concern yourself with it. I realise most women's minds tend to run along that track, they simply can't help themselves it seems, but the more obvious they are, the less—interested I tend to get.'

Davina kept a hold on her temper and replied smoothly. 'I do apologise—I was talking generally but you obviously mistook it for a personal interest in the matter. Perhaps I didn't make myself very clear.'

'Perhaps not,' he drawled.

'Oh, for heaven's sake!' Her temper eluded her. 'Do you seriously imagine I'm now making plans to—somehow inveigle a wedding-ring out of you?'

'You did bring the subject up,' he pointed out. 'And your generalities did have a personal touch, despite your denial. You mentioned my abrasiveness and impossibly high standards——'

'And I should never have opened my mouth,' she said bitterly. 'There are some men who just can't help taking *anything* one says in a personal context. You're obviously a prime example.'

'And you, Mrs Hastings,' he said softly, 'are obviously somewhat intrigued.'

'Oh, no, I'm not,' she countered. 'The very last thing I intend to do with my life, Mr Warwick, is to allow some man to have any say in it—so put that in your pipe and smoke it,' she added, and leant against the door frame with a hand to her brow and a weary look of defiance in her eyes.

Steve Warwick drove in silence for about five minutes. Then he said, 'So, he was a right bastard?'

Davina looked out of her window.

'How did he get you in in the first place?'

'How do they all——?' She stopped and clenched her teeth. 'Please, don't say any more.'

'OK.' He shrugged good-humouredly. 'There's one thing we haven't discussed—your time off.'

'I don't need any set time off.'

'What about your photography?'

'What I usually do on these jobs is just take the time when it comes, if it comes.'

'I see.'

'You don't approve?'

'I'd be a fool not to approve,' he replied drily, and turned the Land Rover off the road and across the cattle-grid.

'Thank you very much for the tour,' Davina said stiffly. 'Would you care to let me know your plans for the rest of the day? Will you be home for lunch et cetera, in other words?'

Steve Warwick pulled the Land Rover up beside the house and turned to her with all the wicked mockery he was capable of glinting in his hazel eyes. 'Do you know how that sounded?' he queried. 'Like a much-maligned wife conducting a domestic dispute with her errant husband—we'll have to watch ourselves, Mrs Hastings. Uh—I'll be home for dinner, so you can have the rest of the day to yourself. Well, you and Maeve, my cleaning lady, that is. Good luck with her.' He leant over to open her door and added, 'Off you go, Davina. I know you'd love to hit me, but if I know Maeve she'll be spying on us from *somewhere*.'

CHAPTER THREE

'I ALWAYS say to people that Mr Warwick is a lovely, lovely man. I know! I know he can be a bit hard to handle sometimes, but he's really dependable.'

Davina drew a deep breath and stared a little helplessly at Steve Warwick's cleaning lady, who resembled nothing so much as a talking, walking beach ball, from her round red face to her round, brightly clad figure. 'Well, I wouldn't know yet,' she murmured.

'Take it from me, luv,' Maeve confided. She had not, in fact, stopped talking since they'd met an hour ago. 'Now, is there any china you'd like me to get out and dust off? Mrs Warwick—that's his grandmother—she's got an eye like an eagle. She could see a speck of dust on them rafters.' Maeve looked upwards and pointed. 'So——'

'No, no thank you,' Davina said hastily and looked around a little wildly. 'Uh—oh, yes, I'd like their bathrooms to be polished up if you wouldn't mind, Maeve. Then perhaps you could start the ironing. I've aired some sheets for them on the line, I'd like them to go through the Elna Press.'

'Certainly!' Maeve said with a wide smile. 'I love that machine. Takes an awful lot of the slog out of ironing. See what I mean about him, Davina? Mr Warwick? It'd be a lucky wife who got him; there's not a thing to make housekeeping easier he hasn't thought of!' And with this further paean of praise she rolled upstairs with bucket and mop and an assortment of cleaning agents.

Davina breathed a sigh of relief and made herself a cup of coffee. She also darted a barbed thought at Maeve's Mr Warwick who could have warned her beyond simply wishing her good luck, she felt—added to all the other things she felt about him. But, as the day wore on, she got more used to Maeve's ways and found that as long as she wasn't given anything too delicate to do, she was a tower of strength. She even cleaned and shone the barbecue which had been neglected since its last use with vigour and much good will.

All the same, when she left at three o'clock, the peace and silence was like a blessing. Davina walked around the house and decided it was nearly perfect and also decided that she was hot, it was a beautiful day, and she'd like nothing more than a swim. So she put her togs on beneath short white shorts and a shirt, stowed a beach towel in the carrier of the bike she chose, donned a helmet and set off towards Blinky Beach.

It was sheer magic pedalling through the golden afternoon with green, green grassy fields leading down towards the lagoon on one side and wooded hills rising on the other. She passed a dell of agapanthas and had to stop and simply gaze at their blue and white heads tossing gently in the breeze. She also couldn't help but feel glad that Steve Warwick had chosen the almost deserted southern end of the island for his house because the feeling of space and aloneness didn't disturb her at all now.

Past the airport she discovered a swamp full of bird-life alongside a paddock of contented cows and she made two resolutions: never to leave home without her camera again, and to buy a book so that she'd be able to identify all the birds.

There was the inevitable bike rack at the bottom of the steps that led over the grassy slope to Blinkys, with several bikes in it and she added hers to it with a slight smile. The beach, she discovered, was perfect. A long crescent of fine sand beneath the almost limitless blue sky, bordered at each end by rocky outcrops and with a decent surf rolling in. The few people on it looked tiny and insignificant and she wasted no time.

The water was delicious, cold and bracing at first but, once you were in, marvellously refreshing. She was a good swimmer and enjoyed surfing and she must have spent half an hour playing in and under the waves before she caught a roller back to the beach, and stood up with water cascading off her and wiping it out of her eyes to come face to face with Steve Warwick.

'Why, Davina.' His hazel eyes laughed at her. 'I thought it might be you!'

She took in, in one swift look, his bare chest, his black board-shorts, the freckles on his arms and legs, his lean, hard physique, and said the first thing that came to mind, 'What are *you* doing here?'

'The same as you, my lovely mermaid, the same as you,' he drawled, but there was nothing swift in the way his gaze lingered on her figure beneath her pink swimsuit and he smiled as his eyes met hers again. 'I've come to cool off in other words. I often do on the way home in the afternoon. Although, you're looking at me as if there should be a law against it,' he mused.

'There should be a law against the way you're looking at me,' she retorted fiercely.

'Sorry,' he murmured, but his eyes laughed at her again. 'I think we've been through this before, I'm talking about the—er—men will be men syndrome. Is that a good way of putting it?'

Davina opened her mouth but decided to storm off instead, something she was unsuccessful in simply because he put out a hand, took one of hers in it so that she couldn't free herself, and said in a different voice entirely, 'No, let's not ruin a beautiful afternoon like this, Davina. Come in and have another swim. I need a break and I wouldn't be surprised if you did too.'

She tightened her mouth but out of the corner of her eye noticed that a couple strolling along the beach had stopped and were watching them interestedly. 'Damn,' she muttered, and then, 'All right, but you don't have to hang on to me as if I was a prisoner.'

So she had another swim and was perversely pleased that she was able to go out as far he did and do everything he did but of course, pride often comes before a fall she was to remember later. Her downfall came in the form of a dumper which caught them both by surprise but he reacted faster and, with all the strength he was capable of, grabbed her just as she was about to cartwheel into the sand and held her safe in his arms as the wave surged beneath them. He then coasted gently into the shore, still holding her. They lay together in the shallows as she spluttered a bit and took some deep breaths to restore air to her lungs.

'Davina?' he said after a few moments.

'Mmm...?'

'OK?'

'Yes,' she panted. 'Thanks—I haven't been dumped for years.'

'That's why Blinkys can be a bit tricky sometimes.'

'I believe you.' She stopped abruptly, and her eyes widened as she realised she was lying cradled against Steve Warwick with gentle wavelets washing up to their waists, and realised that her body fitted against his as if it had been made for it, that their legs had somehow got entwined and that she felt wet and silky where their skin touched, protected and safe in the circle of his arms yet with every inch of her body aware of his and stirred by that awareness. And, finally, aware that she was not alone in this reaction...

They parted by mutual consent, and wordlessly, a bare few moments later. But, while Steve Warwick released her and helped her up and did so expressionlessly, she felt a torrent of colour rushing up beneath her skin and her movements were a bit uncoordinated. She also turned abruptly to walk back up the beach but he said quietly, 'No. At least rinse the sand off you. I'm in need of another swim.'

He swam for at least ten minutes although she just dipped herself and walked back to her towel. But as she dried the moisture from her body and her hair, she couldn't help wondering how she was ever going to face him again. How, for that matter, he would be when he came out... She pulled her shirt and shorts on with unsteady hands.

He was perfectly normal. He made no mention of the fact that it had taken ten minutes of vigorous exercise in cold water to get himself in control—in fact all he said was, 'What's for dinner?'

'R-roast beef. Oh! I'd better get going——'

'Relax. It's over an hour to dinner-time. Isn't that plenty of time to roast a piece of beef?'

'Yes, but I've still got to get there and there's one hill between here and your house that needs to be walked up,' she retorted with more spirit.

He dried himself briefly and dragged on a T-shirt. 'Then I am the answer to all your problems, Mrs Hastings,' he said with humour as his head emerged.

Davina tensed and he narrowed his eyes slightly as he stuck his arms through the sleeves. 'I've got a bike rack on the back of the Land Rover, that's all.'

She bit her lip.

Davina went straight into the kitchen when they got to the house to put the meat on and while she was at it, got the vegetables ready and made her other preparations.

Steve came into the kitchen as she was rinsing her hands. He'd showered and changed into long twill trousers and a blue open-necked shirt. 'All in hand?'

'Yes.'

'Then why don't you have a shower while I make us a drink?'

Davina faced him with uncertainty and wariness clouding her violet eyes. 'I think I'd rather——'

'Davina, I'm thirty-five,' he interrupted pleasantly. 'Which means to say I've had plenty of experience at practising self-control—if that's what you're worried about now.'

She blushed. For the life of her she couldn't help it and at the same time felt a streak of anger because she'd been so hoping he would continue to act as if what had happened on the beach hadn't happened at all. To make matters worse, she could think of nothing to say.

'Go on,' he said mildly, after a moment. 'Unless you're proposing that we avoid each other entirely for a month?'

She went with a toss of her head that brought a faint smile to his lips.

It took her twenty minutes to shower, wash her hair and blow dry it and get dressed into a loose, sleeveless, chalky blue cotton dress that floated around her as she walked. And, all the while, she sought rather desperately for some composure, but it was hard to beat the hollow feeling she had that she couldn't blame her employer for the events on the beach because it was one of those things that had happened quite spontaneously—and mutually.

'How did you get on with Maeve?'

Davina contemplated her drink then looked through the windows to where rays from the setting sun were playing on her favourite mountains and a faint smile curved her lips. 'You might have warned me.'

'You might have run away.'

She laughed. 'No, not really. Once we got to know each other we worked well together. Uh—how do your grandmother and stepmother get on with her?'

'They both keep urging me to get rid of her. They both get totally frustrated by her, not that Maeve notices at all, but the result is general chaos.'

'I can imagine,' Davina murmured and raised an eyebrow at him. 'So, you've stuck with her through thick and thin?'

'Her mother used to work for my mother and her husband, now deceased, worked on one of our boats. I would feel guilty for the rest of my life if I abandoned Maeve.'

'She certainly is a great fan of yours,' Davina commented.

'That probably surprised you,' he replied, with a glinting little smile.

Davina didn't answer but sipped her drink then put it down. 'Dinner should be ready in about fifteen minutes. Where would you like to eat it? Here?' She gestured to the dining setting across the room. 'Or——'

'Here,' he said. 'Why waste the view? I'll set the table—you weren't planning to abandon *me* to dining alone, were you?'

He only set one end of the big glass-topped table but he did it quite artistically and he opened a bottle of red wine.

'That's not necessary—for me, I mean,' she said when she saw it as she put a silver dish down, loaded with roast beef with faintly pink juices running from it, roast potatoes, pumpkin and sweet potatoes. She also had on the tray she'd brought from the kitchen cauliflower *au gratin*, gravy and some wonderfully risen Yorkshire puddings.

'Hell,' he said, ignoring her comment entirely as he gazed with genuine admiration at the puddings, 'and you whipped this all up in a matter of minutes!'

'I've had plenty of practice,' she said with a grimace. 'Would you like to carve or shall I?'

'I will. Do sit down, Mrs Hastings—what's that old saying about the way to a man's heart?' He picked up the carving knife and fork, looking gravely attentive.

Davina sat and said quite calmly, 'But we've spoken of that before and both agreed it's not on, haven't we, Mr Warwick?'

He put the fork into the meat and sliced one slice of beautiful, just rare roast beef before he said, 'We may have, Davina, but other things have spoken for themselves.'

She took up her as yet empty wine glass and examined the pattern on the crystal. 'I think—I'm sure—we should put that down to a momentary aberration.' And her violet eyes were level and cool as she looked at him across the table.

'Well, you're certainly a lot more composed about it now,' he commented, and returned to carving the beef.

She gritted her teeth but forbore to reply. Instead, she rose to serve the vegetables and she was still silent as he poured two glasses of wine, without consulting her. Which left her thinking he really was impossible. But as she was to discover more and more, just when you thought Steve Warwick was impossible, he had a habit of turning the tables. He did so then...

'Tell me about your photography.'

She hesitated then with a slight shrug began to do so. And he listened attentively while she explained how she'd always been fascinated by light and shade, by juxtaposing unlikely subjects and capturing them on film.

'So it's been a lifelong ambition?' he said after a bit. 'How come you got sidetracked into catering?'

'That was my mother. She insisted I have some "solid" qualifications, as she put it, behind me. She's the kind of person who thinks that being artistic in any way is all very well but not much to fall back on when the chips are down—she was right, as it happened, although what she'd had in mind for me was starting my own business that catered for very exclusive parties for the rich and famous.'

'But I should imagine you have a flair for it anyway.' He put his knife and fork together and pushed his plate away. 'That was absolutely delicious.'

'I do enjoy cooking,' Davina agreed as she did the same and picked up her glass. But as he offered to top it up she said, 'No, no more, thank you. I was going to make a pudding but ran out of time. I've prepared a cheese-board and fruit instead.'

'That'll be fine but don't rush. How come the chips came to be down?' He looked at her quite seriously across the table.

Davina looked away and finished the last of her wine. 'I'd rather not go into that.'

'Sometimes it helps,' he commented.

'With a perfect stranger? I doubt it.'

'We're not exactly perfect strangers. On the other hand, strangers can have a less—biased view of things.'

'Why do you really want to know?' she said, at last. 'Anyway, it's nothing earth-shattering and I'm quite happy the way I am, believe it or not.' She smiled faintly.

He lay back in his chair and regarded her thoughtfully. 'Marriage to someone who thought you were a frigid bitch, which, incidentally, we've now *proved* you're not, must have been a bit devastating.'

A faint smile lit Davina's eyes. 'I think it was more devastating for him than it was for me.'

Steve Warwick took his time digesting this. 'So, it was an act?' he said at last.

'Not entirely. He certainly didn't turn me on—for want of a more elegant phrase.'

'Were you forced into marrying him?'

'I was ... conned,' Davina said meditatively, then she sighed. 'You remind me of the Spanish Inquisition in velvet gloves. So, if it will set your mind at rest, my father was faced with the prospect of bankruptcy, my ex-husband was the guy who could either bring it all about or save him, I was the price he asked to take the latter course. There you are.' She smiled at Steve Warwick but not with her eyes. 'You have it in a nutshell.'

'And after you'd done the deed you discovered it wasn't all that simple?' he queried perceptively after a moment.

'After I'd done the deed I discovered ... well, eventually, that my parents were still going to go bankrupt.'

'He reneged, in other words?'

She shrugged. 'He was one of the crop of entrepreneurial millionaires who popped up all over Australia at the time with about as much substance to them as a pack of cards. He crashed like a pack of cards too,' she said dispassionately.

Steve Warwick acknowledged this phenomenon with a grimace and a faint frown in his eyes and Davina knew he was trying to place the name and she held her breath for a moment but all he said was, 'So he conned your father as well?'

Davina traced a pattern on the tablecloth with her finger. 'My father was desperate. So was my mother—desperate about how it was all affecting my father's health, and right to be. He died of a heart attack.'

'I'm sorry. Was that when you—released yourself from the marriage?'

'Yes, more or less.'

'How old were you when you got conned into this marriage?'

'Twenty,' she said briefly.

'How old was he?'

'Forty. But a very fit and young-looking forty, I'll give him that.'

'How did you first come to his notice?'

Davina narrowed her eyes and glanced at him coolly. 'At a ball.'

'Where else?' Steve Warwick murmured, looking wry.

'What do you mean?'

'My dear Davina, you in a ballgown...' He shrugged.

She closed her eyes for a moment and remembered the gown. It had been black and strapless and had fitted her like a glove. She'd also worn long white gloves with it and a choker of pearls... And she remembered the sick feeling that had started to grow in the pit of her stomach as she'd realised her mistake, that she'd have been far better off to wear sackcloth and ashes rather than display herself in a ballgown to a man who stripped her naked with world-weary, cynical brown eyes in a way that left no doubt he meant to have her in his bed by hook or by crook.

She stood up abruptly. 'Yes, well, there you have it, Mr Warwick, but I'm afraid "show and tell" time is over. I'll bring the cheese.'

'So you've hated all men ever since?' he queried softly, making no physical effort to detain her, but managing to do so all the same.

'Yes,' she said through her teeth but added, 'I certainly don't trust them and if you're about to lecture me on the folly of making sweeping generalisations like that, please don't waste your time or mine!'

'I wouldn't dream of it!' He stood up. 'A lot of people prefer to enjoy their misery.'

Davina stilled with her hands around the silver platter, and was briefly tempted to hurl the remains of the roast at him. She said instead, coldly, 'But I'm not miserable, that's what you don't seem to understand. Not all women can only find fulfilment in the arms of some man, and before you take that the wrong way——'

'I wouldn't dream of doing that, either,' he said with his lips quirking, 'but before this *discussion* gets out of hand, I think I'll forgo the pleasures of your cheese-board if you'll forgive me—I have some work to do—but I wouldn't say no to a cup of coffee. I'll be in the study.'

Davina stared at his tall frame with narrowed, frustrated eyes as he walked away, and counted to ten beneath her breath.

They had no further conversation that evening, beyond the basics, and she retired to her chalet feeling thankful but curiously wrought-up. It took a while to fall asleep.

'Have the rest of the day off, Davina.'

It was nine-thirty in the morning, a beautiful cloudless morning with sunlight sparkling on the sea.

'Oh, that's not——'

'Look, just do it,' Steve Warwick said irritably as he stood in the kitchen doorway juggling his car-keys. It had been obvious from their first encounter of the day at breakfast that he was not in a good mood—at least, he'd been terse and preoccupied. 'You might not get another opportunity,' he continued, 'and from the look of the place it's all hunkydory.' He looked around, but not as if his clean, gleaming home gave him much pleasure. 'I'm eating out tonight, anyway.'

'Well...'

'And lunching out,' he said sardonically and added, 'If you would care to have a precise timetable of my movements today, I'm also——'

'Don't bother,' Davina said shortly and turned away to hide the anger in her eyes.

'It is what you wanted to know yesterday, however,' he said cuttingly.

She swung back to him, her violet eyes cool and ironic now, as she said, 'Only in the interests of doing my job, Mr Warwick. You could go to...the moon today, for all I care.'

'And you can go to hell too, Mrs Hastings, which is what you really wished for me,' he replied and walked away leaving Davina with her mouth open for two reasons. Because he was right; she had been sorely tempted to tell him to go to a hotter nether region and because it was unbelievable how things had a habit of boiling up between them...

Not, she thought, as she sat down at the kitchen table rather suddenly, that I could be accused of starting the hostilities today. It's really no wonder he hasn't married, he's got to be the most temperamental man, it surely can't just be me that arouses this reaction? Can it?

She stared at nothing for about two minutes, then shook herself and tried to direct her thoughts elsewhere—such as what she was going to do with the day. And she remembered a little booklet she'd found in her chalet called *The Rambler's Guide to Lord Howe*, and went to get it.

Which was how, half an hour later with some sandwiches, a drink and her camera packed into a back-pack,
she embarked on the Goat House walk up Mount
Lidgbird. She'd chosen it because it was described as the
next best thing to climbing Mount Gower, which you
couldn't do without a guide, and because it sounded too
taxing for an eight-year-old. Halfway up, she saw that
they were right. It was very steep, the path was very
narrow and littered with roots, it was slightly slippery
from the rain of two days ago and, because of the dense
foliage and cover, she felt almost as if she were ex-
ploring some Amazonian rain forest. It was difficult to
find anywhere to stand her tripod, so rough was the
terrain, but anyway the lack of light was a problem so
she contented herself with simply getting to the top.

But once out of the forest, with the grey, bare, basalt
upper cliffs of Mount Lidgbird before her, it became
intensely worth the effort. She stopped for lunch beneath those eerie cliffs, perched on a clump of grass at
an acute angle and admired the northward view of Lord
Howe as it lay literally at her feet. The crescent-shaped
lagoon side of the island with its turquoise water towards
Malabar and Mount Eliza and the rocky, bay-studded
eastern side. She could pick out Steve Warwick's house
and the airstrip and Intermediate and Transit Hills in
between. She could see birds wheeling over the wrinkled
blue of the ocean and hear them calling.

She consulted her rambler's guide before making the
final assault on the actual Goat House cave and then
climbed and edged and hung on by her finger nails until
she made it. She discovered the view was even better
from the shallow cave in the cliffside but the stench of
goat manure was rather overpowering, although there

was not a goat to be seen. She stopped to take some photos before edging round on a tiny path with a sheer drop beneath her until she gasped with sheer delight as Ball's Pyramid to the south-east came into view, floating just like a storybook castle in a sea of pale blue shimmering ocean.

It then became necessary to find a niche where she could sit in some comfort and get her tripod set securely. That done, not exactly comfortably but the best she could manage, she lost herself in trying to capture the marvellous spectacle spread out before her. And when she'd finally filmed enough of Ball's Pyramid and the western side of Lord Howe and the birds wheeling and patrolling the cliffs, she consulted her guide again and turned her attention to some of the plants only found at this altitude like the mountain rose and bush orchid, the island apple and pumpkin tree, most of which were sturdy, twiggy and squat as befitted their station in life—clinging to the side of an exposed mountain.

She started to inch her way back at last, feeling a glorious sense of adventure, space and fulfilment—to be greeted by a sight that made it all flee rather suddenly. Dark clouds coming from the west that looked set to deposit heavy rain on the island.

She swore beneath her breath. The path had been tortuous, steep and slippery enough on the way up; it would be impossible in pouring rain...

But that was what happened. A little less than halfway down the rain came, the already limited light was further reduced and the path became a ribbon of mud. I'll get lost, she thought in some panic. At *least* that, if I don't slip and break a leg or fall down the cliff and kill myself; as it is I'm a mess already. She sat on a rock and grimaced down at herself, liberally coated in mud already from places where the only viable way to proceed had been on her bottom. And, she thought, they're right when they say very steep places are harder to come down than get up...

She took some deep breaths and looked around at the dark, silent, dripping jungle. Even in full daylight, such as it had been on the way up, the path itself wasn't well defined and she'd had to depend on the red arrows nailed to trees or the splotches of red paint on their trunks that were guide marks—now she couldn't even see them. She closed her eyes, then suddenly remembered she always carried a torch in her camera-bag, so she fished it out, felt slightly comforted by its yellow beam—and told herself with gritted teeth that she *could* do this, very, very slowly and carefully.

She did, but it took her nearly four hours, which was double the time it had taken her to get up, and when she finally came to the end of the walk and out into blessed flat open only about a quarter of a mile from the house, she was exhausted, aching in every muscle, limping, sodden and looking rather like a chocolate soldier. It was half-past six, she saw as she forced herself to go on—if she stopped she might stay stopped, she thought. But hopefully I'll avoid my employer, she also thought; he'll probably be gone by now...

He wasn't. As she limped up the drive she was bathed in a pair of headlights—Steve Warwick driving down it in the Land Rover.

He pulled up abruptly and jumped down without turning the lights off.

Davina halted in her tracks and sighed heavily. It was still raining.

He said reverently, stopping a foot in front of her, 'Holy mackerel! Is that really you, Mrs Hastings?'

She gritted her teeth. 'It is indeed, Mr Warwick, and I'd appreciate it if you didn't say another word!'

'Right.' That was all he said but, although he retraced his steps to the Land Rover, it was only to turn the lights off, then he loped towards her again and quite silently picked her up, ignoring the discomfort of her back-pack to both him and her, and headed for the house with her in his arms.

Davina gasped. 'What are you doing?'

She felt his chest jolt and knew it was with laughter. 'Am I allowed to speak?' he queried.

'Yes.'

'I'm going to deposit you in the laundry where you can strip your clothes off with impunity and make use of the shower there to get all the mud off yourself without worrying about fouling up any of your impeccable bathrooms, then I shall convey you to your chalet where we can check you out for any damage. Any queries?'

Davina bit her lip because it was exactly the course of action she'd planned. The shower recess in the laundry had obviously been put there for these kinds of occasions. But she said, 'You don't have to... have anything to do with it, Mr Warwick, however. I'm not significantly damaged, only a bit stiff and sore——'

'Well, Davina,' he broke in, 'I'm afraid you're just going to have to accept my having something to do with it. The alternative might not appeal to you.'

'W-what alternative?'

'The one,' he said pleasantly, 'where I lose my temper and tell you that only a bloody idiot would get caught on Mount Lidgbird in this kind of weather because you could kill yourself that way, and where I tell you *never* to go off like that again without leaving some indication of your plans because I was just about to mount a search-and-rescue operation.' And, so saying, he shouldered the laundry door open, put her on her feet and switched the light on.

Davina swayed unsteadily where she stood, her poor strained knees showed an alarming tendency to buckle, and shock darkened her eyes. 'But... but,' she stammered, 'why should you have worried about me? For all you know I might have... I might have... just stayed out for dinner or something like that.' She stopped and he put his hands about her waist as she swayed again.

'I thought of that, but you would hardly have walked and all the bikes are here as well as the other Land Rover. Besides which, I had this intuition,' he said drily. 'Now will you take your clothes off or shall I?'

'Don't you dare,' she retorted, but with not a great deal of menace, and raised her hands to deal with her shirt buttons only to realise she still had her back-pack on. She made a frustrated sound and was horrified to discover she had tears of exasperation in her eyes. 'Just go away, will you?' she begged. 'I simply can't cope with *you* and all this at the same time!'

Steve Warwick surveyed her sodden, dirty, bedraggled person for a moment then said, with a twist of his lips, 'Don't feel embarrassed, Davina. I've never seen anyone look half as good as you do in the circumstances. I'll get you a drink while you have a shower. I'll bring it to your chalet.' And he left.

CHAPTER FOUR

THE warm water of the shower gushing over her body did improve things physically, she discovered, although she was still going darkly over Steve Warwick's last words in her mind. What had he meant? That her vanity was wounded? Well, he was quite wrong; the very last thing she cared about was how she looked in his eyes and...so what had *she* meant? she pondered, tilting her face to the water. That I hate to look a fool in his eyes? The kind of fool who takes silly risks?

Probably, she acknowledged gloomily, and stepped out of the shower to wrap herself in a thick bath-towel—there was nothing else. And it's just as well the linen cupboard is in the laundry, she reflected, otherwise...oh, damn! What a day. I've still got to get back to my chalet and face him—in a bath-towel.

But she was grateful for the sense of irritation that all this provoked as she filled a laundry tub and dropped her clothes in to soak. Just let him say a word!

He said several. He was in fact waiting for her, as he'd promised, with two drinks. 'Still a drowned rat but a clean one. Care to tell me exactly what did happen, Mrs Hastings?'

Davina clutched the towel closer. 'Would you mind very much if I put some clothes on first?'

'Be my guest,' he murmured.

She tossed her wet head and went into the bedroom and closed the door firmly, thinking, I suppose I do owe him an explanation but he'd better not make too many wisecracks—I just could bite!

She came out five minutes later wearing jeans and a jumper, her hair brushed and her eyes cool.

'Thanks,' she said quietly, as he rose and handed her a drink and waited until she'd sunk gratefully into a chair before sitting down himself and stretching his long legs out. 'I'll make this brief because I've just remembered your dinner-date,' she continued. 'I climbed up to the Goat House this morning in absolutely perfect weather and the views were so wonderful up there I must have stayed for a couple of hours taking photos and it wasn't until I started down that I realised the weather had changed—from the eastern side you couldn't see it,' she said with a little gesture, and sipped some heavenly brandy.

'No, you wouldn't.'

'I'm glad you agree,' she said with irony, then grimaced. 'All the same I'm—sorry to have worried you unnecessarily.' The brandy and soda was working its way down and she laid her head back thankfully.

'Where were you when it started to rain?'

'About three-quarters of the way up.'

'Davina,' he said compellingly, and waiting until she lifted her head and looked into his grim hazel eyes, 'you do realise you *could* have killed yourself, don't you?'

She sat up then stood up convulsively and put her glass down with a snap. 'Look, I've spent the last four hours virtually *crawling* down Mount Lidgbird on my hands and knees—backwards, terrified I'd get lost and fall down a precipice—*of course* I realise...all sorts of things, nor am I proud of anything, it was just——' her voice rose '—one of those unfortunate things that happened!

Why don't you...take yourself off to your dinner, Steve Warwick,' she spat, 'so *I* can get myself something to eat and go to bed!' She turned away furiously.

'I've cancelled my dinner.'

'Oh, hell,' she muttered wearily, all the fire draining from her, leaving her feeling as limp as a wet rag, and turned back to find him standing right behind her. Her eyes widened as she looked up into his and her lips parted to say she knew not what but *something* because the moment had suddenly become incredibly charged, and in the second before it happened, she equally suddenly knew why.

'Don't,' she whispered.

But he did. He took her in his arms, pressed her head firmly into his shoulder and simply held her close. And, after a few moments of shock, her stunned mind made the startling discovery that it was exactly what she needed to still the horrors of the past few hours, to soothe the insidious trembling that had started to rise in her body which was probably only a natural reaction, but all the same... Just some human warmth and comfort, she thought dazedly as she gradually relaxed against him and started to let go. But not much later it began to dawn on her it wasn't any old human warmth and comfort she was enjoying and being healed by—it was the unique blend of warmth and protection that Steve Warwick's arms had offered her before, and only the day before... But how can it be? she wondered, anguished, and moved her cheek restlessly against his shirt. All I want to do is attack him and just this morning all he wanted to do was more or less the same...

She swallowed and lifted her head and framed her lips to say something about being fine now but, as their gazes caught and held, she was arrested and all the fine hairs on her body stood up because she knew she was about to be kissed, and knew there was not a thing she could do about it but, worse, wasn't sure if she wanted to, anyway.

But I must, she thought, and her lips parted and her lashes fluttered agitatedly, causing a cool, absent smile to twist Steve Warwick's lips as he murmured, 'This won't hurt in the slightest.'

'I ... that's not ...' But she got no further, as he bent her slightly backwards over his arm and slid his fingers through her hair, and his lips sought not her own at first but the satiny hollows at the base of her throat—and surprise held her stock-still for a moment. Why? she wondered dazedly. Because it was infinitely tantalising? Because it made her so aware of the curves and hollows of her body and aware that to have him touch her most secret, sensitive places, if he did it with this light, caressing touch, would create a kind of rapture that would have her reeling with delight and ready to do anything for him ...? But how could a man as forthright and often bloody-minded as he was, as strong and powerful, be so ...? She couldn't put it into words, she found, but her lips parted again in wonder and this time he did claim her mouth and his hand left her hair and both hands moved on her body in what felt like all the right places, stroking, gathering her closer, but never once compelling. And she moved into him as she'd been once before and felt the softness of her breasts press against his chest, her hips touch his—and all the while he kissed her more and more deeply.

So when it ended she was as breathless as if she'd run a mile and he was breathing unsteadily too, as he watched her reaction with half-lowered lids and his long fingers traced a devastating little path of delight round her ear and down the slender column of her neck.

She closed her eyes in disbelief that *any* man could do this to her, let alone *this* one, and said huskily, 'After *all* the things you said, how could you...?' She opened her eyes and he was so close that she could see the faint freckles on his skin, the little lines beside his mouth, the way his tawny hair grew from his forehead, the clever eyes.

A glint that was part mockery, part amusement lit those eyes as he spoke. 'You said a few, too, Mrs Hastings, you said quite a few. You also kissed me back and it quite felt to me as if your body was revelling in the closeness we shared.' His hazel gaze dropped to her breasts as if he knew without fear of contradiction how tight and expectant they felt.

Davina gasped, then with a sudden movement wrenched herself out of his arms. 'So I did—I must be mad——'

'No,' he said consideringly. 'Not——'

But she'd had enough. 'Yes, *mad*,' she said bitterly. 'I don't like you and you don't like me. I don't *want* to... to get into anything with you or anyone else. Why can't you just believe that and leave me alone!'

He crossed his arms and laughed at her silently. Which so incensed her that she went to hit him once again but missed when he dodged leisurely and drawled, 'You are protesting a lot, Davina.'

'I hate you,' she whispered, clenching her fists and hating herself for being in this impossible position as well as giving way to ridiculously violent impulses. 'Will you go away and let me go to bed?'

He lifted a lazy eyebrow and his eyes were still full of wicked, soul-searing amusement. 'That could be an unhappy experience alone, but on top of an empty stomach, dear me, you don't have to do that to yourself.' He picked up his drink, moved to the door, opened it and waited. 'Bring your drink; I'll make you something to eat.'

'*Eat*?' she repeated in outrage.

'Yes, eat,' he murmured. 'Since you've decided we don't like each other and I gather you've placed what just happened in the realms of temporary insanity— strange how it keeps happening,' he said gravely, 'but I don't see why we shouldn't at least eat and drink if nothing else, Mrs Hastings. Perhaps I should also warn you that I won't take no for an answer.'

He said it quite lightly but there was no amusement that she could discern in his expression now and she'd seen the prelude to irritation and impatience in his eyes too often before not to recognise it now. 'You wouldn't,' she said, but uncertainly, and she could have shot herself for it.

'I would—look, I'm starving, too, so don't make me pick you up and carry you there, Davina. That would be quite childish.'

'You're... you are...' She gritted her teeth.

'I know,' he agreed. 'Coming?' He smiled as she tossed her head but picked up her drink and stepped towards the door.

'What's funny now?' she enquired as she passed him.

'I knew you were going to do that, toss your head like a bad-tempered, but thoroughly classy racehorse with wonderful lines,' he said gently.

Davina stopped. 'If you say one more word along *those* lines, I shall...probably scream,' she threatened with extreme frustration.

He grinned down at her. 'Sorry, ma'am. I'll try to reform,' he said meekly.

Davina took a breath but let it out without adding anything because Steve Warwick *was* impossible and she had not the slightest idea how to handle him now, she realised. Nor could she help feeling a bit foolish, a bit like a shrew and—and by far the worst part, desperately confused.

'Come into the den,' he said, as they got to the house. 'It's cosier in there in this kind of weather.'

'All right,' she said quietly, 'but I could make us something to eat. I'm not that exhausted and whatever.'

'You look it,' he commented. 'Just do as you're told. Read the paper or something; I'll top up your drink.'

Davina subsided into the leather couch that was warm and supple and beautifully sprung and picked up the paper. The den was an entirely masculine room, with tartan covers on the two wing chairs either side of the couch, a television set, bookshelves and photos of all the Warwick boats on the walls, yet it was cosier in the lamplight on a night like this without the wall of windows in the lounge dining-area. But she found she wasn't interested in the paper and she laid her head back, nursed her drink and stared at the ceiling and listened to the rain beating on the roof.

Why did I do it? she wondered bleakly. Why does it feel so right, in other words? It never has before...

'Here we are.'

She sat up as Steve put a tray down on the low table in front of the settee and drew up a tartan chair. 'Not up to your standard, I'm afraid.'

She grimaced and said wryly, 'Not bad, all the same.' There were two grilled steaks, baked potatoes in their jackets topped with cream, a tossed salad and warm buttered rolls on the tray. Also, the unfinished bottle of red wine from the night before.

'Can you eat on your lap?'

She nodded and sniffed appreciatively. And indeed, the steak was of the melt-in-the-mouth variety and she polished the lot off. 'That beef,' she said, 'is the best I've tasted for years.'

'It's island beef.'

'Must be the wonderful pasture—oh, I can do that,' she said as he rose and took her plate.

'No, you won't—drink your wine,' he ordered, loading the tray and leaving the room with it.

Davina shrugged and sat back with her wine which was a full-bodied Hunter Valley red, but smooth as silk on the palate, something she hadn't fully appreciated the night before. 'Why do I get the feeling I was destined to finish this bottle of wine come hell or high water?' she murmured to herself. 'Which is another way of querying whether Steve Warwick *always* gets his own way?'

'Nearly always,' he replied, coming back into the den silently.

She coloured and bit her lip.

He grimaced. 'I gather I wasn't supposed to hear that.'

'You gather right,' she said evenly.

He sat down again and raised his own glass. 'Well—where do we go from here, Mrs Hastings?' He drained the glass.

'Nowhere,' she said flatly and wearily.

'So, are you saying we ignore the sort of spontaneous combustion we seem to generate?' He lifted an eyebrow at her.

'Yes.'

'And just hope it doesn't keep happening?'

'It won't. Look.' She sat forward and realised she was all but reeling with tiredness now and that two glasses of wine on top of a brandy hadn't helped. 'I can't really think straight at the moment, but——' she moved her shoulders helplessly ' —well I can't.'

'I can,' he said softly. 'But what I think might not please you much.'

'I've no doubt about that.'

He looked amused. 'All the same, for what it's worth, and despite what we've both *said* on the subject, it's not going to just go away. Now if you actually think this state of affairs pleases *me*, I have to tell you it couldn't have happened at a more awkward time for me——'

'Dear, oh dear!' Davina said with a flash of her more usual spirit.

'Yes, funny that,' he mused. 'I mean, how one can't help feeling piqued in certain circumstances. 'Are you?' he queried quizzically.

'I *wasn't* . . .' Davina closed her mouth and felt some telltale heat begin to rise up her throat.

'It's all right, don't let it upset you,' he said gravely. 'I'm quite familiar with the feeling myself—probably only human nature. However . . .' He paused. 'I really don't think it will help to simply pretend to ignore this situation, Davina. We should try to...hammer it out, if you like, make some decisions. Otherwise, life will be extremely trying for both of us for the next month, don't you agree?' He lifted a wry eyebrow at her.

Davina stared at him in silence for about a minute. Then she said hollowly, 'I can see it's not a matter of great seriousness for you——'

'I can assure you it is.'

'No, it's *not*,' she flung at him angrily. 'You're treating it as some kind of *joke* at the moment.'

'You didn't think I was *seriously* unpleasant to you this morning?' He raised an eyebrow.

'I think you can be seriously unpleasant at the drop of a hat——' She stopped and looked at him uncertainly. 'You mean you were...like that...because...?' She couldn't go on.

He nodded and moved his shoulders ruefully. 'I spent a rather uncomfortable night,' he murmured. 'What about you?'

She looked away and put her hands together awkwardly but said nothing.

He studied her averted profile then he said in quite a different voice, 'Did he ever—beat you up?'

She blinked rapidly. 'No, not exactly.'

'Was he your first lover?'

'Yes...'

'And you've decided to make him your last,' he said a little flatly.

'No,' Davina said barely audibly and looked at him at last out of shadowed but steady violet eyes. 'But I have decided, and I've already told you this, that I will never willingly put myself in the position where I'm in any way beholden to a man again.'

He was silent for a time as they gazed at each other, until he said thoughtfully, 'It needn't necessarily be that way, Davina. In fact I think you and I would deal rather well together—I'm a little allergic myself to being beholden to anyone.'

'That doesn't mean to say you wouldn't expect it of a woman you were—sleeping with, let alone a wife—and before you take that the wrong way, I gather anything permanent is not what you had in mind for us—I'm not angling——'

'I know, don't get all worked up again.'

She sighed, then said, 'Well?'

'Well,' he repeated, 'I guess this is it—you're trying to say that outside of my arms the thought of sleeping with me doesn't appeal because you've been hurt and frightened once, whereas I'm trying to say——' he paused and narrowed his eyes '—that when two people attract each other the way we do it's not likely to be either a hurtful or frightening experience, something like that.' He paused again and focused those clever, hazel eyes on her. 'But I've got the feeling there's only one way I'll be able to prove that to you.'

Davina trembled beneath his gaze, knowing exactly what he meant, but at the same time she was struck by an inner truth she hadn't acknowledged since her disastrous marriage. She desperately lacked love in her life and not only the physical side of it, but the warmth, friendship, tenderness and permanence she'd once believed in then lost faith in altogether, or so she'd thought. And where is that here? she mused. How can I know whether this difficult, dangerous, arrogant man is any more prepared to fall in love with me than I am with him? How can I know if those things could exist be-

tween us; there's little evidence of them in his life now
or that there ever was—no, so far there's little difference
between him and Darren, who was prepared to lie and
cheat, so desperate was he to get me into his bed. No,
I'd be mad to expose myself to it again, to...lust, I guess,
even if I seem to suffer from it, too.

'It's no good,' she said huskily, and rose a little unsteadily. 'I'm sorry but if we...make that decision that
it's just not on, it will fade, it has to.' She rubbed her
brow wearily. 'Not to mention the sheer logistics of it,'
she added with some irony.

'You mean how to explain to my grandmother and
my stepmother that I'm sleeping with my housekeeper?'
he said with a touch of irritable sarcasm.

'*Yes*,' she said tautly.

'I never allow them to dictate anything to me, Davina,'
he said coolly.

'Well, bully for you,' she murmured. 'I, on the other
hand, have distinct reservations about sleeping with the
boss when I'm on a job.'

'May I return your sentiment?' he said. 'But I have
to point out you're also splitting hairs.'

Davina raised her hands and moved to the doorway.
'Do me a favour—*you* were the one who said we should
hammer this out; well, we have—at least *I* have, and
you're just going to have to accept it! You were *also* the
one who said it couldn't have happened at a worse time
for you—why don't you take that thought to bed with
you?'

'And what will you take with you?' he said softly,
eyeing her with all the mockery he was capable of.

'Steve...' She stopped, because his name, which she'd
sworn never to use, had risen to her lips unconsciously

and, worse, she'd uttered it as a plea. She closed her eyes but it was too late to deny it. 'Please,' she whispered, her lips suddenly trembling, 'let it be.'

He stood up at last and came over to her and leant his shoulders against the doorframe and the lines of his face were suddenly more serious than she'd ever seen them, as he said, after a moment, 'Are you really sure about this, Davina?'

'I...' She licked her lips. 'Yes. I'm sorry.' Her shoulders slumped suddenly. 'But it would...be impossible,' she said, though.

'No more sorry than I am,' he murmured and, taking her by surprise, lifted a hand and touched her face in the lightest gesture. 'All right.' He straightened. 'So be it. You'd better go to bed. Tomorrow will be quite an experience for you, I'm sure.'

She stared at him, still feeling the touch of his fingers on her skin and with sudden uncertainty in her eyes. Then she forced herself to say, 'What...what time do they arrive?'

'About eleven-thirty.' He turned away. 'What you should really do is have a swim tomorrow morning,' he added. 'The cold water will help any bruises you have.'

'I...will. Goodnight.'

'Goodnight, Davina.'

She hesitated for one brief moment, but he'd sounded so completely normal that it seemed pointless to say any more.

She went to bed, if anything more confused than ever.

'And this,' Steve Warwick said the next morning, 'is Candice.'

'Hello, Candice,' Davina said, stifling her surprise. For some reason, she'd expected an ultra-feminine little girl, but the one who stood before her eyeing her aggressively was anything but. She had scraggly long pigtails, glasses, and her outfit of jeans, blouse and running shoes looked as if it had all been pulled through a bush backwards. She also didn't reply to Davina's greeting, but shrugged her thin shoulders and turned away.

'Candy,' Steve's stepmother Loretta protested mildly.

'Don't call me that!'

'But, darling——'

'I agree with Candice,' the elder Mrs Warwick said briskly, speaking for the first time since apparently being struck dumb upon having Davina presented to her. She was a tall, aristocratic as well as energetic-looking lady who wore her age lightly and Davina guessed she must be at least seventy. 'If you wanted to call her Candy you shouldn't have bothered with Candice, although why anyone should want to call to mind something frivolous and sugary like confectionery when naming a child is beyond me.' And she cast her daughter-in-law an old-fashioned look.

It made no impression on Loretta. She too had been visibly taken aback by the temporary housekeeper, widening her sleepy but spectacular dark eyes and blinking her thick dark lashes several times. It was not easy to put an age on Loretta, Davina decided, but quite easy to see how most men, let alone a possibly lonely widower, could fall for her. She was...'luscious' was the word, Davina reflected a little wryly, once again taking in the river of shining black hair, her smooth olive skin and very white teeth, her—and it would be unkind to say blowzy—but undeniably opulent figure clad also in jeans but with a tiny vest top that left little to the imagination. And for the first time since waking up she felt a trickle of amusement run through her at the thought of the kind of fur and feathers that might fly between the two Mrs Warwicks.

'Yes, well, before we resort to armed combat,' Steve Warwick said a little drily, 'may I say that Davina is here to make your holidays entirely worry-free, so please don't even think about anything to do with the house and, if you wouldn't mind, I'll need some help with this.' He gestured to the mountain of luggage that he'd brought in through the back door. 'How the hell you got all this on the plane I'll never know; the limit is supposed to be fourteen kilos.'

'Darling,' Loretta purred, 'what's the use of owning an airline if you can't bend the rules a bit?'

'I disagree entirely with that kind of thinking,' Mrs Warwick senior said. 'Rules should be rules——'

'But we were the only people on the plane, Lavinia,' Loretta pointed out. 'It's not as if I was endangering lives——'

'You weren't to know that, though——'

'I was. I rang and checked—they assured me I could bring as much as I liked.'

'Anyone,' Lavinia Warwick said arctically, 'who requires that amount of luggage for a simple holiday on a simple island needs their head read. Come, Candice,' she added, 'we'll choose our rooms.' And she stalked out of the kitchen with Candice following.

Loretta watched them go and turned to Steve with a smile. 'Your grandmother never changes, does she? And before you say anything this was *her* idea, not mine, darling. But I'll help you with the luggage,' she added kindly.

'You'd help me a lot more, Loretta, if you didn't wind her up——'

'I didn't! I've been as good as gold!' And she smiled a wide, white, sultry smile at him.

'If you think bringing this amount of luggage with you is not winding her up, I know bloody well it is!' Steve Warwick countered scathingly, and appeared to then count to ten just beneath his breath. And Davina thought with an inward grin that she was enjoying this... All the same, she came to his rescue.

'Uh... lunch will be ready in about half an hour, Mrs Warwick. I thought it might be nice to have it on the terrace, it's such a lovely day.'

Loretta turned to her and said warmly, 'What a great idea! I'll just freshen up. Now let me see, I think I can manage these two, Steve.'

He returned to the kitchen when all the luggage had been disposed of looking thoroughly annoyed and muttering, 'Why the bloody hell I put up with them I can't imagine.'

'For the sake of the child?' Davina suggested as she tossed a salad, and bit her lip. 'Sorry, it's got nothing to do with me.'

'You're quite right, nevertheless,' he said moodily and sat down at the table. 'What do you think of her?'

'Candice?'

'Yes, Candice,' he said sardonically. 'She can be a proper horror when she sets her mind to it.'

'If she's had her mother and her grandmother fighting over her ever since she can remember, it's not surprising.'

He grimaced and folded his arms. 'Do you know, my father was a very sane, sensible man, I always thought. How he could have left a mess like this is beyond me.'

'Don't you have any—affection for her?'

'Yes I do,' he said shortly. 'But I'm only a man, Davina, and there are times when even I am at a loss— my father couldn't stop them fighting and how the hell I'm supposed to is, upon occasions, beyond me.'

'Very difficult, I would have to agree, now I've met them,' Davina said.

'Thank you.' He grimaced again.

'You're welcome.' She carried the salad to the fridge then looked around, but everything else was done.

'How do you think you'll cope with her?' he queried, tilting the chair back irritably.

'Only time will tell.'

'You're a fount of wisdom this morning, Mrs Hastings,' he said with soft mockery.

'And you should guard against winding me up, Mr Warwick, or trying to,' she retorted.

He smiled quizzically and opened his mouth, but they both heard footsteps coming down the stairs and his smile deepened to a genuine grin as he stood up with alacrity and murmured, 'I'll leave you to it—by the way, I won't be here for lunch. I've told them so you don't have to worry about it, but I will be back for dinner.' And so saying, he left via the back door, whistling cheerfully.

Davina stared after him frustratedly.

It was Lavinia who came into the kitchen and she got straight to the point. 'How did my grandson hire you, Davina? He made no mention of any such intentions to me,' she said as she walked around the kitchen, examining surfaces and trailing an experimental fingertip along the windowsill.

Davina explained about the agency and mentioned that she'd be serving lunch on the terrace.

'I see. Personally, I'm always happier eating inside; I don't hold with putting oneself at the mercy of bugs, beetles, birds and whatever when one is consuming food, but if you've already——'

'I have,' Davina said quietly.

Lavinia stopped her tour and looked at Davina keenly, which Davina didn't ignore but didn't allow to fluster her at all.

'Hmm, I see,' Lavinia said again. 'So, you know your own mind, Davina? I like that in a person.'

'Thank you,' Davina replied calmly.

Whereupon Lavinia put her head on one side and said thoughtfully, 'You don't look the kind of person to be doing this kind of job, if you don't mind me saying so.'

'All the same, I'm quite good at it,' Davina said with a faint smile.

'How long have you been here?'

'Three days.'

'And you'd never met Steven before?'

'Never.'

'So—he had no idea he was going to get you?'

'None at all, nor was he particularly pleased when he did get me,' Davina said levelly, thinking, If this old lady is fishing in the manner I'm pretty sure she is, I might as well get this over and done with even though it's become less than true in some respects, but all the same... 'He, too, didn't think I looked the right type for the job. But, of course, the proof of these things is always in the pudding, isn't it?'

'Indeed,' Steve Warwick's grandmother said slowly. 'Indeed.' And with the kind of turn around that was rather devastatingly reminiscent of her grandson, added charmingly, 'Do tell me what's for lunch. I'm starving.'

'Uh . . . *quiche lorraine* with a salad, and fruit and ice-cream.'

'Excellent! I'll hurry the other two up, not that it's ever much good hurrying Loretta, she is the most unpunctual, lazy person I know. And, what's more, if she thinks that on this holiday she'll succeed in getting her hooks into Steven, she'll find she's as mistaken as she has been before or I'm a Dutchman.' And, with this stunning parting shot, she left the kitchen regally.

Davina stared after her and blinked dazedly.

CHAPTER FIVE

LUNCH was apparently successful.

Davina declined an invitation to join them, saying she'd already had hers, and got the impression that both Mrs Warwicks were hungry enough to be somewhat mellowed during the meal. Then Loretta took herself upstairs for a short siesta, as she put it; Lavinia took the second Land Rover to see a friend, inviting Candice to join her but she refused surlily, so her grandmother left with a haughty look.

Half an hour later, Davina was aware of Candice mooching around moodily and decided this might be one of the times when she should act as a babysitter.

'Did you bring any games with you, Candice?'

'Like what?'

'Snakes and Ladders, Monopoly—I thought we might play something together.'

'I grew out of Snakes and Ladders years ago,' Candice said scornfully. 'Besides, I don't like playing with grownups. I don't like grown-ups much at all, if you want to know.'

'Is that so? Oh, well, we all have things we like and don't like, I guess.'

A spark of interest lit Candice's eyes behind her glasses. 'Don't you mind if I don't like you?'

'Not at all,' Davina said cheerfully, and walked away.

Ten minutes later, Candice sidled into the laundry where Davina was scrubbing her sand-shoes, trying to rid them of the mud stains they'd collected on Mount Lidgbird, and asked her what she was doing.

Davina explained.

'Well, when you've finished, I suppose we could play something,' Candice said grudgingly. 'I've got nothing else to do and Mum will sleep for hours,' she added darkly. 'She's a night person, she says.'

Davina made no comment, but eyed her shoes critically. 'Something tells me they'll never be the same again,' she murmured. 'Why don't we go for a swim, instead?'

A further spark of interest showed. 'Steve's the only person who takes me swimming,' Candice said. 'When he can tear himself away from work. Mum can't swim and Gran says she's too old. Mum does lie on the beach a lot, though, getting a tan and catching the eye of all the men around. But she hardly ever gets herself wet. I'm not a very good swimmer.'

'I see. I am,' Davina remarked.

'So you'd come right in with me?'

'All the way.'

'OK, if it's what you want.'

They rode to Ned's Beach, and for an hour or so Candice became like any ordinary little girl, giggling and squealing with enjoyment while she clung to Davina and they fed the fish that zoomed in on them as soon as they entered the water, then had some swimming lessons in the gentle swell. Ned's was a protected beach, unlike Blinkys. Then they put their shoes on and went over to inspect the colony of Sooty Terns that made their home among the rocks at the foot of Malabar Hill on the northern end of Ned's Beach.

'It's amazing how close you can get to them, isn't it?'

'Boy!' Candice said admiringly. 'There's hundreds of them.'

'I should have brought my camera,' Davina said ruefully.

They had an ice-cream on the way home, and had just got off their bikes to walk up the last hill when Steve Warwick pulled up behind them.

'Well, girls,' he said lightly, 'I couldn't have come at a better time. What have you two been up to?'

Candice told him enthusiastically as he hitched their bikes on to the back of the Land Rover, and he watched her glowing little face for a moment then raised an eyebrow at Davina. 'You've done well, by the sound of it, Mrs Hastings—my compliments.'

'What does that mean?' Candice asked as she climbed into the back seat.

'Nothing at all,' he replied and drove off.

Davina said nothing at all.

Candice, on encountering her grandmother when they got home, said plenty, however, still in the same enthusiastic vein, and caused that lady to regard Davina thoughtfully.

Which was probably why she wasn't as successful at ducking out of dinner, she reflected later.

'I insist you join us for this meal, Davina,' Lavinia said grandly, sweeping into the kitchen about ten minutes before Davina was due to dish up.

'Thank you, but——'

'But me no buts, my dear. I too am a person who knows my own mind and I'm about to set another place at the table.' She pulled open a drawer and clanked cutlery vigorously. 'Has Steven made any mention of you eating separately?'

'No, it's entirely my own decision, Mrs Warwick. I have certain practices when I'm on a job, and this is one of them.'

Lavinia snorted. 'Then I'll get him to ask you himself.'

'Ask her what?' Steve Warwick strolled into the kitchen.

His grandmother placed her hands on her hips. 'This silly girl insists on eating on her own. I've decided I won't even hear of it.'

'She is the housekeeper; it's probably a fairly common practice for housekeepers not to ——'

'There are housekeepers and housekeepers,' Lavinia interrupted. 'It's perfectly plain to me that Davina is a rather superior kind of housekeeper but, that aside, who are *we* to stand on ceremony?'

'I'm simply slayed by your logic, beloved,' Steve Warwick murmured, and turned to Davina, amusement twisting his lips. 'It's up to you.'

'How can you be so lily-livered, Steven? Tell her to come!'

'Davina.' There was open laughter in his eyes now. 'Could you please see your way to rescuing me from this little *contretemps*?'

Davina breathed exasperatedly. 'Very well.'

'That's my girl,' he murmured, and swung back to his grandmother. 'Happy now?'

'Extremely, although why I had to go to all those lengths—— '

'Come and have a drink, Lavinia,' he interrupted, and led her out of the kitchen.

'Why do *I* have the feeling I've strayed into a madhouse?' Davina muttered to herself.

'Probably because you and I are the only two sane people in the place.'

Davina jumped. Steve was standing right behind her.

'Why do you keep doing that?' she said irately.

'I came back for some ice—I was not creeping up on you, if that's what you thought. But you know, I complimented you on Candice this afternoon—may I now say that to have impressed my grandmother the way you have is...extremely impressive. How did you do it?' He looked at her, his eyes dancing with devilry.

'I...she seems to think I know my own mind, which is something she admires in a person, apparently,' Davina said carefully.

'Well, she's right about that, I can vouch for it,' he said ruefully. 'But I also have the feeling that, were she to know the implacability of...certain of your mental processes, she would take a very different view of things.'

Davina frowned. 'What do you mean?'

'I think,' he drawled, 'I'll let you work that one out for yourself, Mrs Hastings—I see you're no longer wearing your wedding-ring, incidentally.'

Davina glanced down at her hand. 'No. I...no.'

'Well, that might set the cat among the pigeons but— who knows?' And he withdrew the silver ice bucket from the fridge and walked out with it.

Davina stared after him, shook her head dazedly once then thought, It is a madhouse, and you're wrong about one thing—I might be the *only* sane person in it.

The next couple of days proved several things to Davina. While she wouldn't exactly accuse Loretta of being a lousy mother, she was certainly a bit unhandy at it. She seemed not to be aware that if you laid down rules, you needed to stick to them, with the result, or so it appeared to Davina, that a lot of Candice's tantrums arose from sheer confusion. And it appeared to her that Lavinia exploited this quite shamelessly at times. But there was also very genuine affection for the child.

As for the animosity between the two Mrs Warwicks, while Loretta never appeared to be too fazed by her mother-in-law's barbed remarks, she could always be relied upon to retaliate in a lazy yet telling way. But more and more Davina got the feeling that behind Loretta's lazy smile and undoubtedly lazy ways at times there lurked shrewdness and intelligence. Of the fact that she had any intention of converting her mother-in-law to a Dutchman, there was little evidence. At times she amused Steve, at times she exasperated him, but there were no overt displays of trying to engage his interest with a view to matrimony.

So for a few days Davina ran the household successfully, and worked her way discreetly through the minefield of the Lavinia-Loretta saga by taking Candice off their hands as much as possible. She took the little girl on some photographic expeditions, back to Malabar where they shot the Sooty Terns, to the swamp at the Blinkys end of the runway and out on a glass-bottomed boat expedition where they snorkelled together over the coral in the lagoon and marvelled at the fish—and made Davina long to own an underwater camera. Sometimes, they just got off their bikes and sat in the lush grass and absorbed the views and the lovely clear air.

It did dawn on Davina during these days that Lavinia was trying to find out as much as she could about her background, also that she was rather wily about eliciting information. So that, without Davina quite knowing how she'd done it, Lavinia came to know where she'd been to school—and approved—to know that she'd spent six months overseas with her mother when she'd left school—again approved—to know all about her catering course and to know a bit about her photographic ambitions. This she approved of vigorously. She also managed to draw forth Davina's taste in music, literature and art, her knowledge of current affairs and her opinions and she once said that Davina was obviously well-brought-up, well-informed and had most of the ingredients to be a woman of style and perception as well as amazingly capable. But, beyond a lurking amusement at this process, Davina hadn't given it much thought— for one thing she simply hadn't the time. For another, a lot of her spare thoughts seemed to centre around Steve Warwick, to her dismay, but there was nothing she could do about it, she found.

He seemed to have taken her at her word and she was horrified to find herself remembering what he'd said about pique. Was she piqued? Surely not. So what was she...? But that was even harder to deal with, unless, she thought starkly once, you admitted to yourself that you just couldn't forget the feel of his arms, his lips...certainly not when you virtually lived in the same house with him, encountered him several times a day and so could never free yourself from the impact of his strong, streamlined body, his hands... Stop it, she told herself. Just...stop it.

But she got caught more than thinking it once. He came home one day with a fine catch of kingfish; it was a beautiful evening, so she scrapped her plans for a veal casserole for dinner—it would keep anyway—and while he lit the barbecue she filleted the fish and made salads.

They had a wonderful barbecue beneath the Southern Cross. For once, Loretta and Lavinia seemed able to bear each other's presence; Steve asked Candice to help him cook the fish and she grew almost visibly in stature. But Davina was suddenly attacked by a sense of the vastness of the ocean all around them, and her general insignificance in the great plan of things. It came on towards the end of the meal, fortunately, so no one noticed when she got up rather abruptly to clear up; in fact everyone helped. But she was the last to go to bed, or so she thought, and was lingering in the dim, quiet, clean kitchen—lingering because she didn't trust herself to the loneliness of her chalet—when Steve came in.

From the way he raised an eyebrow she guessed he'd thought the same as she: that he was the only one up. He said quite normally, 'Still around, Davina? I'll have to start paying you overtime.'

And she was furious to discover herself pinned to the spot, her heart beating heavily with an intense longing, her body bereft and aching because his hands weren't on it, the remembered feel of his body against her like a blueprint in her mind and upon her skin.

'Something—wrong?' he said, after a long moment, his gaze narrowing and drifting down to her breasts beneath the white T-shirt she wore with blue shorts, to her long bare legs—and, to her supreme embarrassment, she started to bring her arms up to cross them in a defensive gesture that was also a dead giveaway...

'No,' she said, but her voice was hoarse as her hands sank to her sides. She cleared her throat and started to turn away. 'No, nothing. Goodnight.'

'Goodnight, Davina,' he replied, and although she couldn't identify what it was, something in the way he'd said it made her feel sure he'd known exactly what had happened to her.

She locked herself into her chalet and didn't know why. She put her hands to her face and tried to block out Steve Warwick, but it didn't work. She was tormented by so many things about him: the golden hairs on his arms and legs, the tendency to freckles and the way his dark red-brown hair grew. How it had been to lie against him in the shallows at Blinkys and feel the unmistakable response of his body to hers, the rapture and delight of being kissed by him.

She pushed herself away from the door and, to her grim amusement, went to take a cold shower while she wondered how she was going to get through one more day let alone roughly another twenty-one.

She was saved from herself the next day by Steve Warwick at his very worst. It all started when one of his charter boats, due to an error of judgement by the skipper, ran aground and had to have its passengers transferred to another boat, and be towed home.

Despite the fact that no one was really in any danger, there were other boats in the area and the rescue-boat was quickly on the scene, his anger was awesome.

And when the unfortunate skipper came to the house to make his report, Davina, who was baking a cake and biscuits, couldn't help but be in earshot as Steve explained in the coldest, most cutting terms she'd ever heard that the fact that everyone was safe meant nothing, that the potential for a disaster that could ruin not only his business but the reputation of the island as a holiday destination was what mattered ... and so on.

And, when the poor man finally stumbled out, pale and shaken, she couldn't help but feel some sympathy for him—probably because she knew what it was like to be on the receiving end of Steve Warwick's anger and deadly brand of savage sarcasm. Not that she would have dreamt of saying so, but when he proceeded to take out his feelings on them all, she unwittingly intervened.

It was a wet, gloomy afternoon, which was why she'd decided to make more of a ritual of afternoon tea than usual. Lavinia sampled the cake, pronounced it mouth-watering and said, 'Steve would like some of this.' Steve was still closeted in his study.

Loretta looked at her with wry amusement. 'Then we'll nominate you to take it in to him, Lavinia.'

Lavinia glanced at her coldly, but, to her credit, did say, 'I think we should draw straws.'

And before Davina, who'd gone to fetch some hot water, realised what was happening, Candice had taken up the idea and Davina found herself drawing a short straw and then having to ask its significance.

'Thank you,' she said with considerable irony to Loretta and Lavinia. 'If you want my opinion, we should leave him be.'

'Ah, but Lavinia is of the opinion that your wonderful cake might just sweeten him up,' Loretta murmured.

Davina opened her mouth to say that she had good reason to want to stay outside a hundred-mile radius of Steve Warwick, for reasons that had nothing to do with today, but she caught a look echoed in both their eyes that was oddly curious. Damn, she thought, don't tell me they're cottoning on...? And she straightened her shoulders and went to prepare a smaller tray with as much nonchalance as she could muster.

'What's this?'

'Afternoon tea,' Davina said politely in reply to his curt query and, although she couldn't help being a bit taken aback by the harsh lines his face was still set in as he'd looked up from his desk, she couldn't resist adding when she should have just left it with him, 'Your grandmother thought...you'd like some.'

'Well, take no notice of her in future, Davina. I'll tell you what I like and don't. You can take it away. Tea is the last thing I need at the moment,' he added scathingly.

She felt her temper rising and cursed herself for being jockeyed into this position against her better judgement—all of which combined to make her say, with deceptive gentleness, 'Aren't you being a bit childish, Mr Warwick? None of *us* ran your boat aground——'

'And aren't you taking just a little too much upon yourself, Mrs Hastings?' He overrode her swiftly. 'You're only the damned housekeeper, as you so often persist in reminding me!'

By a huge effort of will, as their gazes clashed and a wave of colour came to her cheeks at the insolence and mockery she saw in his eyes, Davina restrained herself and did the only other thing possible. She turned on her heel and walked out, leaving the tea with him, and even managed to look rueful but calm as she walked back into the den.

'Not a good idea?' Loretta queried.

'No. He's still behaving like a spoilt child,' she said cheerfully, and thought privately that she deserved an Oscar. 'We'll just have to ride it out.'

It was Lavinia, after staring at Davina particularly thoughtfully for a moment, who said, 'He does have an awful temper sometimes, but once it's over it's over. He doesn't bear grudges.'

Ah, but I do, Davina thought to herself later. Thank heavens! I'm back to hating him...

Lavinia's prediction was correct, however. The next day he was back to normal, although he didn't apologise to anyone, but it was at dinner that evening that another bombshell exploded.

The meal commenced with a fight.

Loretta sent Candice up to change into a dress rather than the T-shirt she had simply added to her swimmers, causing Candice to tell her mother roundly that she hated her and Lavinia to tell Loretta that it was her duty to see that her only child was correctly attired *before* they came to the table.

But, just when things looked as if they could get out of hand, Steve, who had been delayed by the telephone, arrived, took stock of the situation and said coolly and cuttingly, 'You'll do as you're told, Candice, and you two will stop squabbling because I'm running out of patience, I warn you.'

Everyone subsided and Davina dished up fragrant, delicious lemon chicken on a bed of fluffy white rice.

'You're just a marvellous cook,' Loretta said warmly to her, halfway through the course.

'I have to agree with you there,' Lavinia said, and said it only slightly grudgingly.

Steve murmured, 'Glory be!' but only audibly to Davina who was opposite him. He also smiled into her eyes, the tiniest, wickedest little smile that was gone before anyone could take note of it, at least Davina fervently hoped so because it acted rather like an electric shock on her nerve-ends.

It was Candice who then unwittingly dropped the bombshell. 'How come, if you're a Mrs, you haven't got a ring or a husband, Davina?'

'She's not a Mrs!' Lavinia said decisively.

'She is—Steve called her Mrs Hastings the other day, didn't you, Steve?'

'Here we go—she is actually, she's divorced,' he said mildly to no one in particular, but then sat back and watched his grandmother's reaction.

'Divorced!' Lavinia said right on cue. 'My dear girl! How come?'

Davina stopped eating and wished herself a hundred miles away again, as well as feeling a flicker of annoyance—why was it anyone's business? Why on earth should it be affording Lavinia such consternation? Why, above all, was Steve actually enjoying this? 'It was a mistake,' she said coolly. 'We were...completely ill-suited, as it turned out.' And she resumed eating as if to say, and that's that.

That wasn't that. 'Were you very young?' Lavinia queried.

'Twenty,' Steve said gravely.

'Did he sweep you off your feet—was he a lot older?'

'I...' Davina looked fleetingly into Lavinia's eyes that were the same hazel as her grandson's and sighed inwardly. 'Something like that,' she murmured.

'No children?' the old lady asked autocratically.

'No children,' Davina agreed.

Lavinia was silent for about two minutes as she chewed some chicken thoroughly and apparently chewed the whole matter of Davina's divorce over at the same time, until finally she said, 'Well, I don't hold with it much, I have to be honest, but on the other hand it would be...unChristian to deny that people do make honest mistakes and they shouldn't be penalised for them for the rest of their lives. Someone as lovely as you, too, Davina, would be rather at the mercy of unscrupulous men I would imagine. So—have there been any other men since?'

Davina breathed deeply and put her knife and fork together. 'Mrs Warwick, I must protest——'

'No, there haven't,' Steve Warwick interrupted.

'And how do you know that, Steve?' his grandmother asked of him haughtily.

'I—er—made the same enquiries of Mrs Hastings when she first arrived,' he replied.

'Well, then,' Lavinia said almost genially after a moment's thought, 'I think we can close the subject, Davina. Yes, I think we can. Of course, I'd prefer it not to have happened, but——' she shrugged '—one can't always have everything. Would there be any of that delicious chicken left?'

Davina caught herself staring at the old lady with her mouth open and the thought running through her mind that perhaps all the madness she'd noted a few days before was infectious.

'I would just go with the flow,' Steve remarked barely audibly at that point, and Loretta, who had followed everything with an odd little twinkle in her eye, said, 'Oh, I agree.'

Davina started to say something along the lines of, If I knew what you were all talking about it might help— but she shrugged slightly instead and rose to offer everyone second helpings of the chicken.

It was during dessert that Davina suddenly became aware of who Loretta was. The conversation had, thankfully, become generalised until Steve asked Loretta how business was going.

'Loretta is a dressmaker, Davina,' Lavinia supplied.

Loretta looked at her ruefully. 'I always rack my brains for a way to refute that, but of course it's true.'

'You don't actually make them yourself now, though,' Steve said wryly.

'No——'

'Not...Loretta C?' Davina said suddenly, her eyes widening.

Loretta glowed. 'How marvellously gratifying—and you are quick on the uptake, Davina!'

'I've worn some of your clothes—although not lately,' she said. 'Your ballgowns are stunning.'

'Thank you! I think so too, but it's *lovely* to hear others say so.'

'They also cost an arm and a leg,' Lavinia said primly.

'Quality tends to be expensive.'

'And before we start exchanging hostilities again,' Steve said, rising, 'thank you for a wonderful meal, Davina.' He also had the gall to add, with a perfectly straight face, 'Would I get something thrown at me if I asked for some coffee in my study?'

Loretta came into the kitchen just as Davina had finished cleaning up for the night. From the sounds she could hear, Lavinia and Candice were watching television in the den and Steve was apparently still working in his study.

'Is it too late to make myself a last cuppa?' Loretta asked.

'Not at all!' Davina smiled at her. 'I'm not some ogre of a housekeeper.'

Loretta grinned back. 'Why don't you join me, then? It's such a balmy night we could sit outside.'

That's what they did, and after some idle conversation, Loretta said, 'I'm really glad you're not an ogre of a housekeeper because I do need this break and, as you may have noticed, I've spent a lot of it sleeping so far. I have to admit,' she said ruefully, 'that given the opportunity I can be a right slob!'

'Well, I think that's partly why I'm here...uh.' Davina grimaced in the darkness. 'I mean to say, at least I can take Candice off your hands a bit.'

'Darling, that was beautifully diplomatic,' Loretta replied with a gurgle of laughter, 'but we all know Steve thinks I'm a lousy mother and unfortunately, in some respects, he's right.'

Thinking, What can you say to that? Davina preserved a tactful silence. She'd also been gradually making the discovery that it was hard not to like Loretta.

'Mind you,' Loretta went on, 'you could have knocked me down with a feather when he presented us with you— had you two not known each other at all, before?'

'Not at all,' Davina said with another, hopefully hidden, grimace.

'Strange,' Loretta murmured, and raised her arms lazily above her head. 'You do realise Lavinia is sizing you up as wife material for Steve, don't you?'

Davina all but dropped her cup. 'What do you mean?' she said in an oddly strangled sort of voice.

Loretta chuckled. 'Darling, Lavinia has two main ambitions in life—one, to find Steve a wife, and two—to make sure it isn't me.'

'But...but...that's unbelievable!' But as soon as she said it, a lot of little things fell into place. 'So *that's* what she was on about over my divorce and everything else, and he *knew* ...' She stopped abruptly.

'Exactly. I really felt for you when you looked so mystified. It must have been rather like the Mad Hatter's tea-party.'

'But surely you can't make those kind of decisions on such a short acquaintance? Lavinia's known me for barely five days.'

'Lavinia can, believe it,' Loretta said drily. 'What's more, once she's made them, she *never* changes her mind. Contrary to what they all might tell you, I made her son exceedingly happy in the short time we had together— oh, yes, I did spend quite a bit of his money, but mainly to set myself up as a dress designer and I'm now earning it back very nicely. Nor did I wear him into an early grave; the condition he had that ended his life was there before we ever met. But none of the aforementioned has ever persuaded Lavinia that I am anything but a slut.'

'Did *he* make *you* happy—I'm sorry, that was unforgivable.'

But Loretta merely smiled. 'As a matter of fact, he did. But I'm an honest person, unfortunately, I sometimes think, and I'm no good without a man in my life. I've neither attempted to stay celibate since he died, nor could I conceive of doing so in the future.'

'Why...why does she think you...want Steve?' Davina said after a long pause.

Loretta thought for a while. 'Well, let's be honest again,' she said at last. 'Few women in their right minds would not want Steve, and I have to confess there've been times when I've thought—there's no law against it. But, of course, I could never be the woman *Steve* wanted and not only because of his father.'

'Why not, apart from that?'

Loretta glinted a fleeting white grin across at her and said gently, 'I don't think you're an inexperienced little girl, Davina, for all that we may be quite different types apparently. Falling in love with Steve Warwick,' she went on deliberately, 'would be part heaven, part hell, don't you think? Unless you were prepared to be owned body and soul—I'm not that kind of woman.'

'Who is?' Davina said very quietly, and felt a tremor pass through her.

'Oh, I think it can happen, although not often. Those kind of all-or-nothing love-affairs, I mean. You're probably a little cynical after your divorce,' she added, and sent Davina an uncharacteristically acute little glance.

'Aren't you?' Davina queried. 'A little cynical, I mean? Isn't that what you've been saying, up to a point?'

'No,' Loretta mused, 'I've been trying to be honest. In other words, I know myself rather well.'

Davina was silent for a long time, then she made an effort and said, 'I still can't believe his grandmother could seriously—well, want to promote anything between us. She really can have no idea whether I'm a...heaven alone knows what!'

'Ah, well.' Loretta shrugged. 'I'd be surprised if you were.'

Davina took a breath and made a swift decision to try to lighten things up. 'Don't you start,' she said with an attempt at light, wry humour.

Loretta raised her hands. 'Wouldn't dream of it—by the way, I must thank you for winning Candy around the way you have. I was beginning to think it wasn't possible!'

'It was actually surprisingly easy, but then I think it often is with children, for outsiders.'

'That could be true,' Loretta said slowly. 'I must say it amazes me that the actual fact of motherhood doesn't automatically equip one with all the right responses. Still, I do keep trying. You know, I would *love* to dress you, Davina,' she added, changing the subject completely. 'You have the most divine figure, you're tall enough to carry most clothes—how tall are you?'

'Five foot eight—I thought one had to be a bit taller——'

'No, no, there aren't many Jerry Halls out there; five foot eight is fine. For what I had in mind for you,' she said mischievously.

'The problem would be paying for them,' Davina said wryly.

'Did you not get anything from your ex-husband?' Loretta enquired curiously.

Davina smiled. 'Not a cent. He was declared bankrupt, you see. I was only lucky I wasn't involved in any of his ventures, otherwise I could have met the same fate, so——'

'Oh, I wouldn't expect you to pay for them! Just wear them, as an advertisement kind of thing.'

'That's very kind of you——'

'No, it's not!' Loretta protested vigorously. 'Believe me, it happens all the time and it's good business sense.'

'Well——' Davina hesitated, a bit taken aback as she perceived that Loretta was deadly serious '—but then there's the problem that I don't go anywhere where anyone would see me.'

'Ah.' Loretta lay back and chewed her lip, but not for long. 'People will see you here, though.'

'Here?' Davina regarded her quizzically.

'It's amazing how many very interesting people come to Lord Howe, despite its laid-back aura, Davina,' Loretta said seriously. 'Because it's so unique, you see. In fact, it's a seriously trendy sort of place to come if you want to prove you're into the *untrendy* ... if you know what I mean. World heritage stuff and all that kind of thing. I've seen premiers and even one Prime Minister here, television, film and radio stars—you'd be amazed how many well-known people come here——'

'Stop!' Davina said with a laugh. 'I believe you. But you seem to forget, I'm only the housekeeper, so I'm still not going to be seen where all these seriously untrendy trendies gather——'

Loretta sat up. 'You don't know Lavinia!' she said earnestly. 'She is, among all the other things she is, a great socialiser. I think she also regards herself as the Queen Mum of Lord Howe. Give her a few more days and she will have winkled out enough people to have a party, if not many parties!'

'Oh, God,' Davina murmured with genuine reverence. 'The mind boggles.'

Loretta chuckled. 'I know what you mean.'

'But all the same——' Davina stood up '—I'm still only the housekeeper and I don't suppose you came armed with a wardrobe full of clothes for me, so, look, thank you,' she said warmly, 'I appreciate the thought, but it just couldn't work.'

Loretta subsided. 'A problem,' she admitted.

'Well, I think I better take myself to bed, it sounds as if I'm going to need to conserve my strength. Goodnight.' Davina got up and stretched, but asked then, curiously, 'Why doesn't Lavinia live here if that's how she feels about the place?'

'The winters are too severe for her; it can be pretty cold and windy. She lives in Queensland now, where they're very mild. She also likes to terrorise some of the other family operations on the mainland.'

'So...' Davina stopped, but Loretta read her thoughts. She said, 'Yes, Steve's father left him quite an impressive empire and Candice a slice of it all, too. There are also a couple of manufacturing plants that Lavinia actually brought into the family, which is why she regards them as her prerogative.' Loretta grimaced. 'I often think that's why Steve lives here, although he has to spend a lot of time over there, of course. But this is undoubtedly his favourite home. His father used to tell me how he loathed being sent away to school. And that's another thing.' She sat up again. 'They're great believers in higher education, the Warwicks—the finest schools and so on, and I can feel the pressure building up for me to send Candy away to boarding-school soon. I can't help feeling,' she said with a sigh, 'that that might alienate Candy from me forever. You know it really would solve a lot of my problems if Steve married and had kids of his own—I'm sure Lavinia would get off my back then!'

'I'm definitely going to bed now,' Davina said ruefully.

'Oh, well, there are other contenders, and one right here on the island, I'll have to get to work on her,' Loretta said humorously. 'Night!'

But bed wasn't what she really wanted, Davina decided, once she was in the privacy of her chalet, because once again she felt restless and keyed up—probably from all the revelations of the evening—and would toss and turn for a while, she just knew. She sighed, then took her trusty torch from her camera-bag and decided to see if a walk would help.

It was a magnificent starry night and she crossed the road and walked through a paddock to its grassy edge above the beach on the lagoon side where the tide lapped gently against the sand and rocks. She'd noticed a bench there from the road during the day and swung her torch to locate it. She did, about twenty feet away, but there was someone there before her, someone who stood up and revealed himself as Steve Warwick.

'Oh, no,' she said wearily. 'I mean—sorry, I didn't mean to disturb you. I'll go——'

'You aren't. Disturbing me, and there's no reason for you to go. I always find it's particularly relaxing to have a stroll before bedtime and to enjoy the peace and quiet. I should imagine it's been quite an evening for you.'

'You're not wrong there,' she murmured, but still standing as if poised for flight.

He smiled slightly in the torchlight. 'Put it out and sit down, Davina, I'm not going to eat you.'

She hesitated then sat and he sat down beside her. But she was as taut as a piano wire and it was impossible to project any other image.

'What's wrong?' he said after a few moments.

'I . . . nothing really.'

'Sure?' He raised an eyebrow. 'You haven't been having any further discussions with my grandmother on your suitability as—a bride for me?'

Davina shuddered and turned to him. 'You *knew*,' she accused. 'And laughed!'

He shrugged his broad shoulders. 'I have to confess I found it rather amusing in the light of what had happened between us. Wouldn't you—if you could be a fly on the wall?'

'Would that I could,' Davina said bitterly. 'I still don't understand *why*. She must make your life hell if she . . . goes about doing this all the time.'

He grinned briefly. 'I have a thick hide—if it's any consolation she was probably spurred on this time by Loretta's presence. She has an absolute horror of . . . that happening. So you have been talking to her again?'

'No.'

'Then how did you work it all out?'

'Loretta told me.'

'Ah.' He said no more.

'What does that mean?' Davina asked reluctantly.

'Loretta's no fool,' he answered almost absently. 'What else did she tell you?'

Davina blinked. 'Nothing much. Well, she asked me to advertise some clothes for her but we were able to sort out that it wasn't practical or indeed possible—I feel,' she said, with a sudden tremor in her voice, 'a bit like Alice in Wonderland. Yes, as if I've fallen down a hole.' And she put her hands to her face suddenly.

Steve Warwick made a slight movement but stilled it. 'Perhaps you ought to go to bed,' he said rather drily then. 'Come, I'll walk you back.' And he stood up and held his hand out to her.

Davina dropped her hands and looked up at him but his expression was unfathomable. Then she looked at his hand, but instead of putting hers into it, stood up unaided. 'Sorry,' she said very quietly as they turned and started to walk towards the house. 'I'm not usually this . . . whatever it is.'

'I should imagine there's one thing that's not helping,' he said, and his voice was dry again.

'What?' she asked uncertainly.

'When two people know they could find—solace and a release in each other's arms, to have to cope with denying that as well . . .' He shrugged.

'You . . . you promised,' Davina said huskily and stumbled so that this time he just took her hand with an impatient sound. They weren't far from the bottom of his driveway.

'I'm not doing anything,' he said roughly. 'Merely commenting.'

'If you had any . . . if you were any sort of a——'

'Gentleman?' he supplied.

'*Yes*. You wouldn't even comment——'

'I don't know that being honest is not being gentlemanly,' he said irritably. 'Do women honestly prefer the latter to the former?'

She took a breath and decided to ignore this. 'What makes you so sure about the release and solace and not, for example, all sorts of turmoil and trauma?' she queried starkly.

He stopped walking and turned her to face him. 'Can I tell you some things about yourself, Davina?' He didn't wait as she opened her mouth to protest. 'You're twenty-five, you were never made to sleep alone all your life— OK, so you have some cause to be bitter and wary, but I can picture you before it all happened. I can picture you as being warm and generous and full of life as well as intelligent and spirited. Do you know what's left? A beautiful face and figure—and an overburdened spirit that's often caustic and sometimes downright sour. And *all* because you're heaping the sins of one man on all of us. Do you know the only times when the old you shines through? When you're photographing or talking about it, and when you're with Candice,' he said significantly. 'You're like a different person.'

She stared up into his hooded eyes for a long moment. Then she said, 'Damn you, Steve Warwick. You've got no idea what it's like to be virtually raped on your wedding night, so don't preach to me.'

'You shouldn't have married him, Davina.'

'There's one little detail I forgot to mention,' she said curtly. 'Not only was my father likely to go bankrupt, there was a strong possibility he could go to gaol for misrepresentation to his shareholders—could you have stood by and seen that happen to your father if you'd had the means at hand to prevent it?'

He closed his eyes briefly and sighed. 'Davina, I'm sorry. But, look, even if it's not to be me, don't wear it like a thorny crown for the rest of your life.' And, in another surprising gesture, he raised her hand and kissed her knuckles. 'You'd better go to bed now.' And he turned away abruptly and disappeared into the darkness, away from the house.

She put her knuckles uncertainly to her lips, then turned herself and stumbled up the drive.

CHAPTER SIX

WAS HE right?

The thought crossed Davina's mind time and time again over the next couple of days. And she realised that perhaps what had shaken her most was how Steve Warwick had so accurately captured her 'before' and 'after' image. But the other thing that she had at the back of her mind all the time was the feeling that he'd really washed his hands of her this time—and the little shaft of pain the thought of that brought.

There were certainly no further demonstrations of any interest on his part, not that she saw a great deal of him. But when they did cross paths, he treated her perfectly normally, which was to say, as usual, that depended entirely on his mood. He was certainly not an easy man to live with, although his grandmother and his stepmother would be enough to try the patience of a saint, she caught herself thinking once with a curious mixture of humour and wryness, and caught her breath as she wondered if there wasn't a little streak of tenderness in her thoughts as well.

Fortunately, just as Loretta had predicted, Lavinia did get herself into party mode and decided to kick off the proceedings with a cocktail party for thirty people, a combination of island residents and some very interesting people she'd met, she said.

Does she waylay them on the beach? Davina wondered. Loretta answered that on another occasion.

Apparently, Lavinia consulted the register of the Warwick guest-house for likely candidates. All the same, the preparations for the party gave Davina little time for much else. And little time to notice that Loretta was acting in a slightly mysterious manner—that was to say, she didn't notice at all that Loretta had commandeered the sewing-machine from a laundry cupboard because she'd been unaware of its existence, and was unaware that a lot of the time she supposedly was taking a siesta, Loretta was actually doing something quite different.

In fact, the mystery didn't reveal itself until the afternoon of the party. Davina had wondered if Lavinia would insist she attend and had geared herself to refuse quite categorically but the subject hadn't come up— perhaps Lavinia had assumed it was a *fait accompli*?

Then Loretta came downstairs and into the kitchen at about three o'clock with a pile of violet material in her arms that she held up dramatically to reveal as a dress.

'Oh, that's lovely,' Davina said, as she polished glasses. 'Should suit you beautifully.' And noticed Candice, who was helping her, glance at her strangely. Lavinia was also in the kitchen filling crystal and silver bowls with nuts.

'Not me, *you*!' Loretta said triumphantly.

Davina put down her tea-towel. 'What do you mean?'

'I've altered this dress for you to wear tonight. I've never worn it myself and, contrary to what you believe, my dear Davina, this colour will suit you much better than it would suit me because it matches your eyes almost exactly.'

Davina counted to five then said steadily, 'But I'm not coming to the party, Loretta.'

'Of course you are!' Lavinia intervened. 'Apart from anything else, Loretta has spent so much time making you a dress!'

Davina narrowed her eyes. 'You—don't tell me you two have been in cahoots over this?'

Loretta gurgled. 'Strange, indeed impossible as that sounds, nevertheless it's true.'

Davina rose and said stiffly, 'Well, I'm sorry to have to break up this *entente cordiale* but I'm not coming as a guest, and that's that. For heaven's sake, there's enough to do as it is!' she added feelingly.

'Such as what?' Lavinia enquired. 'The cold snacks are made—so are the hot ones. The chicken wings, savoury pastries and those lovely little sausage rolls you made only need heating up at the right time. Between us, we can cope with that. And Steven is a very good barman!'

'I can help him there,' Candice chimed in. 'He showed me how to pour champagne once.'

'No.'

'Davina!' all three entreated.

'Look,' a different voice said, 'just leave her be.'

They all swung round to see Steve leaning his shoulders against the doorframe and regarding them impatiently.

'Thank you,' Davina murmured.

'But *why*?' Loretta said fervently.

'It's got nothing to do with you, Loretta,' he replied curtly. 'If Davina prefers to be a recluse, that's her affair. As for all this partying,' he turned to his grandmother irritably, 'just don't get carried away, Lavinia, because it's not particularly how I enjoy spending my rather precious time on this island.'

Lavinia snorted. 'You're in some danger of becoming a recluse yourself these days, Steven Warwick!' she retorted.

'Then, beloved, that is entirely my affair, too. Just don't push it, Lavinia,' he warned.

Lavinia sighed frustratedly. 'I had so hoped you'd be in a good mood this evening,' she said mournfully.

'I will be, so long as there's no more of this nonsense.' And he turned to Candice and said lightly, 'What do *you* intend to wear, pumpkin?' Which was an occasional endearment he used that appeared not to faze his prickly half-sister at all. Indeed, she looked gratified and told him that Davina had starched and pressed one of her dresses and promised to blow-dry her hair so that she could wear it loose.

'What would we all do without Davina?' was his only comment, although it was loaded with irony and accompanied by a curiously mocking little look at Davina, not lost on any of them, as he strolled out again.

'He can be *so* difficult sometimes!' his grandmother bemoaned.

'He can also be a right bastard sometimes,' his stepmother reflected.

'Well, I quite like him,' Candice said.

And Davina said abruptly, 'I'll come—please, don't say a word, I've changed my mind, that's all.'

'You have to admit, I'm not bad at what I do! I mean, it was all guesswork really.' Loretta stood back and admired her handiwork.

Davina stared at herself in the mirror and could only agree. The violet dress fitted her perfectly and was perfectly stunning—a taffeta sheath with a loose, slightly fuller overdress of filmy georgette. It just skimmed her knees, had a halter-neck top, a low back and a cyclamen trim that gathered the bodice in and became the ties behind her neck. The combination of the two colours was exciting, the cut and lines were exquisite and the whole thing seemed to flow with her body.

'What do you think?' Loretta asked.

Davina turned to her with a faint smile, 'You're a genius, but it's a bit more revealing than——'

'Perish the thought!' Loretta commanded. 'What's the use of having a figure like yours if you don't make use of it?'

Davina heaved an inward sigh and once again castigated herself for allowing Steve Warwick's mocking look to goad her into trying to prove to him that she wasn't a willing recluse. But the deed was done... 'What are you wearing?'

'Something a lot more revealing, darling,' Loretta purred. 'I mean to say, you can't even see your cleavage and a bit of back is hardly anything shocking!'

'OK! OK—it is a lovely dress and thank you for all the work you've put into it but you shouldn't have.'

'I enjoyed every minute of it. And there are these to go with it.' 'These' were matching suede violet pumps and pale grey tights. 'I've got the feeling we've got the same size feet.' Davina slid her foot into one shoe and nodded. 'So—take half an hour off, relax a bit, and come out looking wonderful,' Loretta commanded. 'Candy has given *me* permission to do her hair and Lavinia is already in her war-paint and revelling in being temporarily in command of the kitchen—I'll leave you to it!' And she waltzed out of the chalet joyfully.

Davina sighed again then slipped out of the dress and went to wash her hair.

An hour later she was ready.

She'd put her hair up loosely and put on a pair of drop pearl earrings, her only jewellery. She'd also used more make-up than she normally wore, some shimmering grey eyeshadow and mascara as well as a film of foundation, but she'd done it all with the lightest touch so that although it was barely perceptible, she felt finished.

Outwardly, that is, she mused as she stared at her reflection in the lovely dress. Inwardly, I feel about as much in a party mood as if I were going to the guillotine in a tumbril—damn! This is ridiculous. Why did I let myself in for it?

Because you wanted to show Steve Warwick something, she answered herself ruefully, and squared her shoulders suddenly and added, so do it.

Lavinia was in the kitchen when Davina returned to the house about twenty minutes before the guests were due to arrive. And, as Loretta had mentioned, she was dressed and ready and looking marvellously regal in black lace with her short cap of silver hair elegantly styled and with a strand of the most exquisite pearls Davina had seen around her neck. Causing her to say, genuinely, 'You look wonderful, Mrs Warwick!'

'Thank you, child,' Lavinia responded and looked down complacently at her lace dress. 'I may not patronise Loretta C, but I didn't get to eighty-two without knowing a thing or two about clothes myself.'

'Eighty-two!' Davina said before she could stop herself.

Lavinia positively glowed. 'Surprised you there, didn't I? I surprise most people—it all comes from healthy living and having a mind of your own. You look very nice yourself, I must say, although—well, no——'

'Say it, Lavinia.' Steve walked into the kitchen and came to stand in front of Davina with his eyebrows raised expressively as he looked her up and down and murmured, 'A change of heart, Mrs Hastings? One could almost say you've gone from the ridiculous to the sublime in that dress.'

Davina knew she was blushing and knew there was not a thing she could do about it, as his gaze moved upwards from the slim length of her legs clad in filmy grey to come to rest briefly on the almost bare skin of her shoulders then clash with her own gaze.

'Well, I was going to say that Loretta sometimes *undresses* people rather than dresses them—heaven alone knows what she will be wearing herself!' Lavinia soldiered on. 'But Davina seems to be able to carry it with dignity, don't you agree, Steven?'

He turned away at last and smiled with genuine amusement at his grandmother. 'Oh, she does.'

For a moment Lavinia looked perplexed—but only for a moment. 'I had thought *you* might wear something more formal, Steven,' she started, but he cut her off with another smile.

'Now, you didn't really, did you, Lavinia?' he mocked. 'When have I ever dressed up for one of your cocktail parties?'

His grandmother regarded his plain white fine lawn open-necked shirt and khaki trousers—all of which had been ironed to perfection by Maeve—his tamed tawny hair and the look of irony in his eyes and said frustratedly, 'Well, what do *you* think, Davina?'

Davina blinked and was conscious that, quite unfairly, Steve Warwick privately took her breath away a little whatever he wore... 'Er...'

'Yes, Davina, what do you think?' he drawled, turning back to her, his eyes alight with sheer devilry.

She bit her lip, and said stiffly, 'It's got nothing to do with me.'

'I thought you might say that,' he replied sweetly. 'There you are, dear Grandmama, it's no good appealing to Davina, she—er—refuses to involve herself with me. So you'll either have to be a lot cleverer or more subtle about whatever you have in mind—do I hear someone arriving?'

Lavinia, who had been looking from Davina to Steve, and particularly at the way Steve hadn't taken his eyes off Davina, with something like dawning comprehension in her own eyes, came to with a start and bustled out of the kitchen so far as anyone as regal as she could ever be said to bustle.

Leaving the two of them alone, and leaving Davina feeling like a mouse in a trap, and hating it. 'Why did you do that?' she hissed, her eyes dark and angry. 'That was as good as telling her... telling her——'

'Telling her the true state of affairs between us, Davina?' he queried softly and moved his shoulders slightly. 'To tell the truth, I don't entirely know why I did it either, but it might have had something to do with you in that dress.' His eyes lingered all the way down her body then came back to hers. 'Be that as it may, do you really think you can hide from them? Loretta and

Lavinia? I have to say I doubt it—why do you think they jockeyed you into this position in the first place? So we might as well have it out in the open and be done with all the innuendoes et cetera. That's what I think,' he said placidly.

'Think what?' Loretta flowed into the kitchen all in silver and, surprisingly, the dress covered her from her neck to her wrists to below her knees, pleated, tissuey, billowing and with not a square inch of exposed bust or back to be seen. And she had a large silver bow binding her black hair.

'I thought you said you were wearing something similar to this——' Davina broke off abruptly and frowned.

'Changed my mind,' Loretta replied laconically. 'There are some things you can't fight, and outshining *you* in certain respects tonight is one of 'em, apart from defeating the purpose—er——' She broke off, looked fleetingly chagrined with herself then turned nonchalantly to Steve and repeated, 'Think what?'

But he was laughing silently at Davina's slightly murderous expression, and it was a moment before he said, 'See what I mean? Loretta,' he added to his stepmother with absolutely false and suddenly assumed gravity, 'you're quite right, Davina and I are going through a bit of hell because we took one look at each other and were wildly intrigued, but to Davina's mind there's absolutely no future in it. So there's *no* need for any further probing little forays to be indulged in between you and Lavinia, not to mention presenting Davina to me rather like a bait on a hook—that is how things stand. Why, pumpkin——' his hazel gaze came to rest beyond Loretta where Candice stood rather shyly in the doorway

'—now you do look like Alice in Wonderland. Can I take you to the party?' And he crossed the room, took Candice's hand in his and led her out, much to her obvious joy.

'*Bastard*,' Loretta muttered as she looked around, plucked a bottle of champagne from a silver cooler, popped the cork with a minimum of fuss and poured a glass of it. 'Here, drink this. Sit down—don't look like that, he's only a man but *they* can be absolute hell sometimes, talking of those things!'

'I...' Davina tried to steady her trembling lips as she did sit down rather suddenly. 'He...how could he?'

'I know,' Loretta said soothingly. 'Come on, have a sip. The thing is,' she went on after Davina had had several sips of champagne, 'you don't have to take anything lying down from him.' She grimaced ruefully and said, 'I didn't mean that literally, but just give him as good as you get! If I were you, I'd give him a right royal run for his money—that's the way to handle them.'

'Talking of running, all I want to do is run away right now,' Davina said hollowly.

But Loretta was outraged. 'Don't you dare! That would be as good as admitting everything he's saying about you is right!'

'I don't...I'm not sure what he is saying...'

Loretta cocked an eyebrow at her. 'That you're a coward?' she suggested softly. 'That's one of their favourite themes,' she added knowledgeably.

'But don't you see?' Davina said distraughtly. 'I just don't want to get into those kind of...pride and ego tussles, or whatever they are, with any man!'

Loretta shrugged. 'How right you are, but——' she paused '—Steve...I've never known him to actually chase a woman like this, and I mean in a no-holds-barred, don't-care-who-knows kind of way. I think you must have affected him rather deeply, Davina.'

'He promised,' Davina said bleakly. 'He promised he'd let it be.'

'Then it looks as if he can't—honey, if I were you I'd think twice about Steve. For all that he can be a bastard, he's got a hell of a lot going for him, and I don't only mean in a material sense. He's a man who would certainly look after you and I can't help thinking you need a bit of looking after.'

'But I want someone to really love me...' Davina stopped desolately, then went on with a shrug. 'All we've done so far is fight. You see——'

But Lavinia swirled into the kitchen at that point and said sternly, 'Come, girls. All our guests are here and it's not their fault that we have a domestic dispute in our midst. I need all hands on deck, now!' And she stalked out.

'*Our* guests!' Loretta marvelled at the same time as Davina said dazedly,

'A domestic dispute!'

They stared at each other until, reluctantly they had to smile. Then Davina sighed, but Loretta said, 'Chin up, chicken! I don't care what you show Steve Warwick, but you're going to show him something tonight! Let's go...'

'You're Davina Smith-Hastings, aren't you?'

It was an hour after she'd been more or less forcibly led into the party and she had to admit it had gone quite well. Lavinia had immediately taken her under her wing and introduced her to people simply as Davina, a friend of ours. But she'd still been sufficiently disturbed not to be able to take in many names or faces, and grateful that everyone she'd met had had a ready supply of small talk. One or two of the women had even commented on her dress and asked her where she'd got such a divine creation. And gradually she'd calmed down and been able to feel like just another guest among the cheerful throng, although she'd given Steve a wide berth. She had not, however, failed to notice a dark, attractive girl in red who appeared to have a slightly proprietorial attitude towards him, and had wondered if this was Loretta's contender from the island. But at all times, for a while, she'd had either Lavinia or Loretta standing by. Now, though, they'd both disappeared, into the kitchen, she guessed, and she was confronting a short, dapper man whose face was vaguely familiar and who had managed to jolt her out of her preoccupation.

'Why?' she said briefly.

'How is Darren?'

A nerve moved in her jaw as she said tautly, 'Who are you?'

'Paul Grainger,' he replied easily. 'We were introduced earlier but I got the feeling the name didn't mean much to you.'

'It does now, Mr Grainger,' she replied coldly, 'and the face. But I refused all your television station's requests for an interview on your programme, and nothing has changed.'

He shrugged. 'Do you know I have a film crew here on the island, Davina?'

'So what?' she said baldly.

'Well we're here to do a documentary on this unique place; I plan to introduce little segments like that into my programme, but it would certainly have—er—some added value if I could capture Darren Smith-Hastings' ex-wife say, cycling around the place. I could even speculate on why she is employed as a housekeeper, your true position with the Warwick family, I believe, although——' he looked her up and down '—one has to wonder whether Steve Warwick mightn't be your next project. Oh, look, there are so many things I could speculate upon. Did you marry Darren for his money, for example? Did you desert a sinking ship when he lost it? I could even put him in touch with you! The last time I interviewed *him*, which was not so long ago—he's making some sort of a comeback—he sounded as if he had a bit of a score to settle with you. He mentioned that you only married him to get your father out of the mire. Or——' he paused '—there is an alternative.'

'What?' Davina said in a strangled voice.

'You could give me an interview, Davina. In some faceless room on the island, so no one would know where you are. And you could tell me all about your turbulent life with Darren Smith-Hastings——'

'I think not,' Steve Warwick said from behind Davina. 'You know, Paul, I've never liked your gutter brand of journalism but this is entirely unethical, and it's with no regret that I must ask you to leave. Moreover, if I find you lurking anywhere around Davina, that is something you *will* regret.'

Paul Grainger stood his ground for nearly a minute then he murmured, 'Well, well—she has got you in. I just hope *you* don't get a touch of the shorts, old man. Goodnight.'

* * *

'Here.'

'No. Don't feed me any drinks, please,' Davina said rather blindly. 'It happens to me too often these days.'

'Sit down, then,' Steve Warwick said and put the brandy he'd poured her on a table beside a couch. They were in the den with the door firmly closed although the party had started to wind down, and he'd got her there with the minimum of fuss.

'You know what's going to happen now, don't you?' Davina said tightly instead of sitting. 'We're going to become an item on his ghastly little social round-up. And the papers will pick it up and...' She did sit down then. 'Now do you understand why I——'

'Yes, but he could have bumped into you on the beach, Davina. So it *was* Darren Smith-Hastings,' he said meditatively. 'I wondered if you'd cut your name in half.'

'So what if I did?' she said shortly.

'Do you think he wants you back—it sounded a bit like dog-in-the-manger stuff, to me.'

'He doesn't,' she said bleakly.

'You seem very sure of that.'

She rubbed her face. 'I am. All he was trying to do, I would imagine, is retain some part of his reputation by coming over as the wronged husband, particularly if he's trying to make a comeback.'

'I see.'

She looked up wearily and stared at him for a moment. Then she said flatly, 'You don't believe me, do you? At best, you're *wondering* about that too now, aren't you?'

'No.'

She got up abruptly and moved restlessly across the room. 'I'll have to leave. I——'

'Davina, I said no.'

'I'll still have to leave,' she murmured impatiently.

'And go where?'

'I don't know, but——'

'So you're afraid Darren Smith-Hastings is likely to pursue you if he finds out where you are, in a mood of—vengeance, say, despite what his public face is?'

She shivered suddenly and whispered before she could stop herself, '*Yes* . . .'

There was silence for a couple of minutes as she stared out of the window through a sudden haze of tears. Then he said, again from right behind her, 'Well, I think in that case your best bet is to throw your lot in with me, my dear. Because, for one thing, he doesn't scare me in the slightest.'

She froze, then turned convulsively, her lips working as she struggled to speak but no sound came, her eyes wide and shocked.

'While, for another thing,' he said barely audibly as he looked down at her and raised a hand to touch her cheek, 'we want each other and there's not a damned thing we can do to change it.'

'No.' She swallowed. 'I mean there is . . .'

'No, you were right the first time, Davina, there's not. Let me show you.' And his arms closed round her and for the life of her, despite her agitation and confusion, it was impossible not to feel safe suddenly.

'Steve . . .'

But he started to kiss her, deeply and searchingly, and his hands moved on her body finding the curve of her waist, the swell of her hips, caressing the bare skin of her back and moulding her to him. Then he moved one hand to her hair and the pins she'd used fell out and he spread his fingers through its thick, silken disarray before he released the halter bow at the back of her neck—and all the while he held her against the strong, hard length of him and kissed her as she'd never been kissed before. So that she was conscious only of him and the intimate plundering that neither hurt nor repelled her but did strange things to the pit of her stomach, as if a slow fire was starting to burn and spread through her whole body. A languorous warmth sparked with a dangerously mounting sense of excitement, a tingling all over her, a sense of relief that she could be made to feel like this after all, and a sense of wonder at the marvellous feel of him against her. A desire to explore him as he was her and feel the muscles of his back and shoulders under her hands, the taut diaphragm, to see her skin against his . . .

But she gasped as he lifted his head at last, gasped a little for breath, but also because she hadn't wanted it to end, and because his long fingers drew the front of her dress away, exposing her breasts.

'Steve . . .' Her eyes were suddenly wary.

But he said, 'Shh . . . I'm not going to hurt you.' Nor did he, as he still held her with an arm around her waist and used his free hand to touch first one nipple then the other and the most exquisite sensation ran through her body.

'Oh, God,' she whispered and tilted her head back, closing her eyes as those fingers strayed briefly to the soft skin beneath her arm and then he bent his head again and trailed his lips down the column of her neck to the valley between her breasts and, once again in turn, took each nipple in his mouth.

'Steve...please...' Her body trembled in his arms with desire and unthinkingly she raised a hand and pressed it through his hair. 'It's too much...'

'Perhaps you're right—for here,' he murmured, raising his head and looking into her eyes. 'But now do you see, Davina?'

She couldn't answer as her lashes fluttered up and down; she couldn't breathe properly, she found. Her pulses were still racing and she yearned for him to touch her again because it had been the sweetest kind of torture she'd ever known, and it was more than torture to have to stop... As the weight of all this hit her, delicate colour flooded her cheeks, her neck and her breasts, and her eyes dilated suddenly.

'Hey,' he said softly. 'Don't for one moment think you're alone. Letting you go now is going to take about every ounce of will-power I possess, but I've just had a thought.' And he moved her slightly away so he could do up her dress. 'There,' he said with a faint, grave smile and his arms still around her. 'Almost proper. Will you be all right if I leave for a few minutes?'

'Y-yes,' she stammered, 'but——'

He kissed her forehead. 'Don't worry about it, and don't go anywhere; I'll be right back.'

He was gone for about fifteen minutes, however. During which time Davina took several minutes to get herself under some sort of control.

She picked up her scattered hair pins from the carpet and tried to put her hair up again, but there was no mirror so she gave up and combed it as best she could with her fingers. Then she noticed the glass of brandy on the table and had to stifle a slightly hysterical bubble of laughter after she'd taken a large swallow of it. Finally, she stood in the middle of the room with her arms protectively around her and thought, Would it be so bad to be looked after for a while? Even by a man who is a mystery in a lot of ways?

And he *is*, she thought with sudden intensity. He may be able to arouse me as no other, but can he ever *love* me? I don't know... I do know he can be hard sometimes, and does he even believe in lifelong love? Why hasn't he found it yet? Is there some secret in his past I don't know about? Why do I get the feeling he could be as cynical in his own way as I am? Does he know that I sometimes feel contaminated...?

The door opened and her eyes jerked to Steve Warwick's in sudden fright.

'What is it?' he said with a frown.

'I...' She cleared her throat. 'What are you going to do? I couldn't——' She stopped uncertainly.

He studied her upturned, pale face for a moment, then his lips twisted. 'Neither could I. So we're going away. Don't worry, I've sorted it all out with that pair of ill-assorted matchmakers. Come.' And he held out his hand to her. 'Or do I have to kiss you again to make you?' he added very quietly.

She blushed, hesitated, but he took her hand and led her out of the den.

'Where are we going?'

'You'll see.'

Davina twisted her hands in her lap and tensed as they approached the turn-off to the airfield but Steve drove past. Tensed because her bag and camera case was on the back seat of the Land Rover with another bag—his, she presumed. To a guest-house, then? she wondered as they drove past Blinkys and on to Lagoon Road. I couldn't stand that, it would be as good as telling the whole world!

But he drove past the last guest-house and in the twilight past Old Settlement Beach and up, it appeared, towards the Catalina crash site. But, as the road petered out and she knew there was only grassy paddock riding up towards the contours of Malabar, he turned off into a driveway almost hidden by huge trees and pulled the Land Rover up before an old small house, nearly lost beneath the Norfolk Pines and Sallywoods surrounding it.

'Please, tell me what this is,' she said breathlessly.

'A retreat,' he said lightly. 'It's the original Warwick dwelling on Lord Howe. Lavinia actually came here as a bride sixty-odd years ago, and lately she's restored it. I'm not sure whether for sentimental reasons or because she's toying with the idea of opening it to the public as an example of how they lived in bygone eras on the island. I don't know if I'd let her do that,' he said meditatively. 'She keeps telling me I have no use for it now I've built the other house but it's nice to come back to sometimes. Come inside and tell me what you think.'

'It's...' Davina stopped and looked around in wonder again, a bit lost for words. Because the cottage—and it was no larger than that and lit with kerosene lamps— was like taking a step back in time. The walls were wooden, vertical pine planks a little uneven in places and stained a warm honey colour. The sitting-room and kitchen were all in one, with a huge fireplace surrounded by cream and pink floral cretonne-covered fat armchairs and sofa at one end and a large black, aggressively polished range at the other. The furniture, dining table and chairs were a mixture of natural and white painted pine and there were tapestry footstools in front of the armchairs, starched white curtains at the window and copper-based lamps with pretty floral glasses around the wicks. There was also a mantel running right round the room about three-quarters of the way up the walls from which pictures hung with their strings exposed in the old-fashioned way, and ornaments sat upon—some of them even Limoges, she thought with a lift of an eyebrow. 'It's wonderful,' she said at last.

'Come and see the bedrooms.'

There were three, and he left the main bedroom to last. Davina caught her breath as he ushered her in ahead of him. Because it was dominated by a beautiful brass and white enamel old four-poster bed that was clothed all in crisp white. A white linen cover edged and trimmed with exquisite handmade lace, white *broderie anglaise-*covered pillows piled up on it and two bedside tables, also covered in white linen skirts with more lace and satin bows and two matching sets of delftware basin and ewer. There were blue and white handwoven rugs on each side of the bed and a marvellous brassbound pine glory-box at the foot of the bed.

She couldn't resist the smile that curved her lips as she surveyed the room.

'Like it?' he queried.

'It's lovely,' she said genuinely. 'But——'

'I know,' he said with a wry lift of his eyebrow. 'Lavinia has gone a bit overboard here. I don't remember this room like this. The laundry and starching work alone involved would be horrific. But I believe it did all belong to my great-grandmother—she just kept it in the box, mostly.'

Davina smiled again and then turned to him with her expression sobering. 'How long...I mean...?' She couldn't go on and moistened her lips.

'How long do I plan to keep you here?' He looked into her eyes, observed the shadows there and reached out absently to tuck a tendril of hair behind her ear. 'Only as long as you want to stay.'

CHAPTER SEVEN

'THEY sent all this?'

'They did indeed.'

Davina was unpacking a carton of food in the kitchen and she hadn't responded to what he'd said only a few minutes ago about how long she would like to stay. Nor had he pressed her. He'd simply taken her hand as he had a habit of doing, and led her back to the kitchen, and then he'd brought their bags and this carton which she hadn't noticed in from the Land Rover.

And her stunned mind had only been able to come up with one thing—perhaps I can make myself useful. But as she unpacked and stowed foodstuffs, eggs, meat, vegetables, bread, fruit, cheese, some of her sausage rolls, biscuits, flour, salt and pepper, butter and cream, even vinegar, mustard, some herbs and spices and several bottles of wine, she said involuntarily, 'There's enough here for a month——' She broke off and bit her lip, then added, 'Well, not really, but—how did they manage in such a short time?'

'Both Loretta and Lavinia, each in their own way, are very determined, capable people. Loretta packed your bag and Lavinia did the food. Candice reminded me to bring your camera.'

'Poor Candice—was she upset?' Davina queried.

'Well, she wasn't absolutely thrilled to be left on her own with those two, but I promised her we'd pick her up and take her swimming and take her out to Ball's

Pyramid in the next day or two. She always loves a trip out there.'

'I think she's quite fond of you.' Davina bent down to a cupboard to put some things away and when she'd straightened he was in the kitchen beside her opening a bottle of wine.

He said, 'And you—how about bread and butter, cheese and your sausage rolls? I'm not that hungry. Are you?'

'No...'

'Nor did you drink much,' he added, reaching for a couple of wine glasses. 'Barely a full glass.'

'How do you know?'

'I was watching you,' he said with a faint smile and offered her a glass of wine. 'Go and curl up on the sofa. I'll bring the rest—unless you'd like to change into something more comfortable?'

Davina looked down at the violet dress and swallowed. 'Later, perhaps.'

He said nothing, but there was a wicked little gleam in his eyes that she knew well. So she took the glass and went down the other end of the room and made a pretence of examining the paintings.

'Do you know what I'd like?' he said about ten minutes later as he brought the warmed-up sausage rolls and a plate of bread and cheese to the table in front of the fireplace.

Davina turned away from a rather good water-colour of Mount Gower. 'No.'

'I'd like to think you trusted me enough to tell me some more about it.'

'You mean my life with Darren?' she said jerkily and moved to sit down with a sigh. 'I don't even want to think about it,' she added barely audibly.

'OK.' He sat down beside her and turned to face her with his arm along the back of the sofa behind her. 'Then should we take up where we left off?'

Davina laid her head back and trembled. 'I...still have some reservations about that.'

'Tell me.' He didn't say it impatiently, but quietly, and reached across and picked up the plate of sausage rolls to offer her one. 'You didn't eat anything, either.'

Davina relaxed a little and bit into one of her feather-light rolls, finished it and took another saying ruefully, 'I didn't realise I was hungry—Steve, do you believe in love?'

He thought for a bit. 'The until-death-do-us-part kind?'

'Yes,' she whispered.

'Yes, but I don't know if it hits you on the head, so to speak,' he said slowly and with an oddly searching look. 'Do you?'

'I...don't know...'

'Don't believe in it or don't know if this is it?'

She shrugged and sipped some wine. 'Both, perhaps but it's...what I have a longing for, despite any impressions I might have given to the contrary.'

'I guess we all do.'

'Do you?' She looked at him over the rim of her glass.

He laid his head back. 'To be honest, it's been there, yes, but it hasn't been a blight on my life. I think it's rather contingent on finding the right person. I thought I had, once,' he reflected. 'She thought otherwise.'

'How do you mean?' Davina asked.

'Well——' He grimaced. 'In the sense that she told me she could no more live most of her life here than she could fly.'

'And that broke you up?' Davina said a little incredulously.

He looked at her wryly. 'It's a fairly major sort of schism, don't you think?'

'But...'

'Are you wondering whether a wife shouldn't automatically cleave unto her husband wherever it is as they did in the bible? I don't think wives quite see themselves that way any more—and it's probably a good thing. Saves a bit of heartache later on.'

Davina drank some more wine. 'What about the girl in red?' she said slowly and decided to be quite honest. 'Loretta told me she was a "contender" and she looked as if that was how she saw herself.'

He said, with a hint of amusement, 'So *you* were watching *me*.'

Davina sighed gently. 'Obliquely, yes.'

He said musingly, 'I've known Mary Hargreaves all my life. She was born here, too, although she left the island for a few years and has only recently returned.' He lifted his eyebrows. 'And returned rather changed.'

'How?'

'She's a lot smarter, a lot more sophisticated, but one thing hasn't changed. She loves Lord Howe.'

'Have you ever considered—falling in love with her?'

'No,' he said briefly.

'Poor girl,' Davina said softly.

'I haven't ever led her on, so to speak.'

You don't need to, Davina thought but didn't say. 'And there's been no one else?' she said instead.

She thought he looked at her rather drily before he said, 'There've been a few affairs down the years; I'm not a monk but neither am I a compulsive womaniser.'

'Steve,' she said slowly, 'why did you—you did try to leave me alone for a while, didn't you?'

'Yes,' he agreed. 'You may have noticed, I'm not the most patient, sympathetic sort of bloke, and I thought...the way I am might not be what you needed— among other things. Like a slightly dented ego,' he said, quite gravely, but she knew he was laughing at himself. 'The thing was,' he went on, 'I found it impossible to live in the same house with you and not to—be able to have you. I'm sorry if that sounds crude, or whatever, and I'm aware,' he said in a different voice, 'that to you it might put me in the same league as Darren Smith-Hastings, but there is at least one difference. I think the feeling is mutual between us.'

'And that's something,' she said in a subdued voice, 'I just can't deny.'

He said no more but took her free hand and pressed her fingers gently.

Davina felt tears sting her eyelids but she battled them and said huskily, presently, 'Thanks for being so honest, anyway. Perhaps I can be the same. I...the thought of having someone like you...to look after me and take charge of my life for the time being, and it has been pretty barren for years now, is almost irresistible. The thought of how I feel when you hold me and kiss me— is the same. But it's almost impossible for me to think beyond that and I have to say that while I long for love and tenderness I'm also a mass of insecurities. I just don't know if I could be any good in bed with anyone now,' she said as lightly as she could. 'So——'

'Why don't you leave that up to me, Davina?'

'But,' she said tensely, 'I feel . . . tainted, sort of. I feel used and old sometimes, you saw it yourself. I . . . he . . .'

'Don't. I can imagine. Can I tell you something?' he said gently, and got rid of her wine glass so he could draw her into his arms. 'On that memorable occasion when I first saw you, when I behaved so badly, it was mainly because my first impression was—how absolutely stunning you were.'

'But you also told me with your eyes——' she breathed '—I mean you might as well have told me I was beddable but that's *all*.'

'I know,' he said wryly. 'I think I must have had some sixth sense about you. An intuition what a thorn in my flesh you were going to be. I also——' he paused thoughtfully '—never like to give way to those very physical first encounters. I've always found it's wiser to be—well, more circumspect. And, you see, it comes as a bit of a shock to most male egos to look at a girl and know immediately that you want her—which makes you quite vulnerable, believe me—whether she's willing or not.'

Davina smiled slightly and grimaced at the same time. 'I bet they're mostly willing, though.'

'Well, that's the other thing.' He ran his fingers down her arm. 'There's this hunter instinct, I guess, plus the desire for a *good* woman who is only going to succumb to *you* eventually, that makes you hope she's not immediately willing.'

'That's—only a man could think like that!'

'I know. We're a difficult breed.'

'Not to mention dangerous.'

'Oh, entirely.' He placed a feather-light kiss on her lips. 'See what I mean?'

She laughed and, in an entirely natural movement, snuggled closer to him. 'I always thought, when we did this—*if* we did this—it would be charged with all sorts of—high drama.'

She didn't see the odd little look he cast the top of her head, she simply laid her cheek on his chest and closed her eyes. He let her be for a few minutes, then he tilted her chin and started to kiss her.

She sat on the white bed some time later in a short satin nightgown with a deep lace V neck and linked her fingers together nervously. She'd had a shower in the old-fashioned bathroom—at least it looked old-fashioned with a tub on claw feet, black and white tiles and an old wooden credenza with the basin let into it, but a thoroughly modern shower cubicle had been installed and the water both gushed and was hot.

She'd brushed her hair and cleaned her teeth and smoothed some moisturiser on to her skin and now she was ready, she hoped. The whole process had only taken a few minutes but she hadn't failed to notice the tension starting to build in her eyes again. Steve had gone outside to deal with a shed door that had started to bang regularly as a wind had risen and rain started to fall.

'Sorry,' he said wryly as he came into the bedroom looking damp and windblown. 'The lock had broken so I had to find something to tie it up with—hey, I knew I shouldn't have left you,' he added, sitting down beside her and looking into her eyes.

She coloured faintly but said, 'That makes me feel like a—wimp.'

'No. Listen, why don't you hop in?' He drew back the bedclothes. 'I'll be with you in two ticks.' And as she slid down, he turned the kerosene lamp right down to barely a flicker.

Davina watched his shadow on the wall then closed her eyes. A few minutes later the other side of the bed sagged as he climbed in beside her and took her straight into his arms. He wore nothing at all but he buried his face in her hair and said, 'If you knew how often I've dreamt about this you would also know that I'm much in need of *some* guidance.'

'What do you mean?' she whispered, taken by surprise.

'You'll have to tell me...' But he stopped as a tremor shook her, and lifted his head to look at her. 'What did ⎺ say wrong?'

'I... it's nothing——'

'Yes, it is, I could feel you withdrawing and I can see you looking frightened again.'

'I told you this might happen,' she said unhappily.

'Well, I think you're going to have to tell me why,' he said gently and frowned as if trying to recall something. 'All I was going to say was that I need you to tell me if I'm going too fast for you, like a bumbling boy.'

She caught her breath as he smiled suddenly with those wicked little glints in his eyes.

'But, I guess it brought back some memories,' he said, suddenly sober. 'Tell me, Davina.'

'He...' She stopped, then made herself go on. 'He used to try to make me talk to him in a... certain way. It was horrible.' And she turned her face into his shoulder.

He held her for a long time. Then he said slowly, 'It's supposed to turn some men on.'

'But not you?' she said in a muffled, but suddenly hopeful voice.

'I can't think of anything I'd like less,' he said quietly, and tilted her face so he could look into her eyes. 'But if I'm ever hurting you or not pleasing you, I'd like you to tell me that. And——' his lips twisted '—I can't deny I wouldn't mind a bit of encouragement now and then, but you could restrict that to... let's see, how about, "I quite liked that, Mr Warwick," or something along those lines?' He raised an enquiring eyebrow at her.

And Davina found herself laughing suddenly. But she said primly, 'Very well, Mr Warwick, I'll do my best.'

He hugged her and they lay together loosely for a while until she felt warm and safe again. And only then, as if he knew instinctively, did he slide her nightgown up over her hip and start to caress her thigh. And, to her immense relief, all the shadows of her past life began to recede until she was aware only of him and the things he did to her body just by touching her with that light touch that both soothed and excited. And when he finally claimed her, she was both wet and welcoming and a little dizzy with delight as she moved beneath him in a rhythm she hadn't known before that seemed to unite them to a final peak of pleasure that rocked them both as if they were one, and affected him as much as it did her.

'Well, well,' he murmured, still breathing a little unevenly as they lay facing each other with their arms around each other. 'So I was right.'

'Right?' She freed a hand and traced the line of his jaw.

'I had the feeling we would do this extremely well together. I just couldn't see how it could be any other way.'

A smile curved Davina's lips. 'It's not very nice to harp on how right one might have been, however,' she said gravely.

'You don't agree?' he queried just as gravely.

'Oh, I agree, Mr Warwick.'

'Then?'

She stared into his hazel eyes and let her fingers drift into his tousled, tawny hair and was suddenly shaken by a rush of emotion. 'How can I say thank you?' she said huskily, and buried herself against him suddenly.

'Don't,' he said very quietly and stroked her hair. 'Don't even think it.'

'It's hard not to. You were... wonderful,' she said softly.

'So were you, so were you. And I never even got your nightgown off,' he said whimsically.

'You'd already had me half undressed earlier on,' she reminded him.

'So I did.' And it seemed as if he was about to say more but in the end didn't and she wondered drowsily why, but she was so comfortable, so *contented*, she thought with some wonder, she was quite happy to lie in his arms and drift slowly towards sleep. Which she did and it took a few days for her to realise just how delicately Steve Warwick was handling their affair, how he always introduced a note of humour into their love-making, how he went out of his way to do nothing to shock her or bring back any memories of the kind of violation she'd suffered before. How he was healing her little by little—and to realise that things couldn't always be that way between a man and a woman, although that was something she was to learn the hard way. But, for the next few days, it was a kind of growing magic...

'It's still raining.'

'I know,' a voice said beside her, and Davina sat up abruptly, stared around confusedly until Steve pulled her down beside him and said with mock reproach, 'Hey! Remember me? The guy you made love to last night?'

'Oh...' She subsided, laughing. 'I wasn't sure where I was—of course I remember you.'

He buried his face in her shoulder. 'Remember me well, I hope.'

'Very well.' She smoothed her hands along his shoulders.

'What I'm trying to establish is whether you remember me kindly enough to repeat the experience in the next few minutes, because I have to tell you that I'm intoxicated by the warm, soft feel of you and the perfume of your skin. I can't keep my hands off you—and it is raining, as you remarked.'

'What's that got to do with it?' Davina enquired with a catch in her voice as he once more slid her nightgown up.

'Well, there's no point getting up, is there?' He spanned her waist with his hands then moved them up to her breasts. 'I think I am going to take this off this time,' he added. 'I feel it might get in my way this morning.'

And, because she was weak with desire and love, she simply sat up and did it herself then slipped down beside him again. 'Does that answer all your questions, Mr

Warwick?' she murmured, as he enfolded her completely naked in his arms.

'Beautifully,' he replied seriously.

That afternoon, despite the soft rain, he found some old waterproofs and they went for a tramp up to the Catalina crash site and he told her the history of it, how the Royal Australian Airforce flying boat in 1948, flying low with a faulty hydraulic system, had clipped the ridge and plummeted down the paddock, and they inspected the wreckage then walked up to the memorial plaque in memory of the men who had died. When they got back, Davina was glowing from the exercise and the fresh misty rain, and Steve stopped to chop some wood for the stove and the fireplace—and the heavens opened again and it started to pour heavily. They were laughing breathlessly as they got inside with bundles of wood and after they'd dried off, Davina turned her attention to cooking dinner on the wood stove. They'd combined breakfast and lunch into one meal, chops and eggs which had been relatively simple to fry, whereas dinner was going to be more complicated...

'But I always wanted to try one,' she assured him as she assembled her ingredients for a beef and burgundy casserole, potatoes Anna and broccoli in a cream sauce.

He watched her working, wearing jeans and a short-sleeved white jumper with an old-fashioned frilly apron complete with bib tied around her. Her hair was loose and the moisture in the air had added to its fullness, and he smiled slightly as she tucked some strands behind her ears and regarded the stove that he had lit thoughtfully. 'I guess one has to guess at the temperatures,' she murmured.

'I guess so,' he agreed, his eyes still on her.

She looked up and an impish light lit her eyes. He, too, had changed, into jeans and a yellow sweater and he looked big and vital, and as if he had other things on his mind. 'You're not going to be much help, are you?'

'I know next to nothing about cooking on one of these; there used to be an electric stove but Lavinia threw it out. Besides which——' he paused and his hazel eyes locked with hers '—I could get into trouble for interfering with the cook. There's something about your apron that is driving me wild.'

'Why don't you go and do something else, then?' she suggested airily but with her pulses beginning to hammer.

'There's nothing else I want to do.' He leant his shoulders against a cupboard and folded his arms.

'Steve,' she tried to say seriously, not quite sure whether he was serious or not, 'I don't take my cooking lightly, so I'm liable to get irritable if—what are you doing?' she queried as he pushed himself away from the cupboard and came to stand right in front of her.

'*I'm* trying to take this rejection lightly,' he murmured.

'It's not a rejection!' she protested. 'But we have to eat.'

'Yes, ma'am.' But he didn't move.

She made an exasperated sound and stood on her toes to kiss him. 'There, will that do?'

He considered. 'If I were to be assured it was only a down-payment, it might.'

'You...oh!' She relaxed as she saw the laughter beginning to lurk in his eyes.

'Had you going there for a bit, didn't I?' he teased.

'Yes, you did,' she retorted, but laughing herself. 'Now, will you leave me in peace, please?'

'Certainly,' he replied promptly, but added, 'When I've done this.' And he took her in his arms and kissed her thoroughly. 'I was only half teasing you, you see,' he said, as she lay flushed and breathless against him.

'You're impossible,' she said huskily, but amended that almost immediately as he stroked her hair. 'If anyone had told me you could be like this when we first met, I wouldn't have believed them.'

'Like what?'

'So... nice,' she said barely audibly. 'So much fun to be with.'

He grimaced slightly. 'Has it occurred to you that we might bring out the best in each *other*?'

She lifted her eyes to his and they stared at each other for a long moment. 'I didn't know I could be fun to be with any more,' she said uncertainly.

'Well, you are, take it from me,' he said in what she later thought might have been a deliberate lightening of the moment, and couldn't help wondering why.

But at the time, when he went on to say that if she was serious about wanting to cook them dinner now might be the time to start just in case she was instrumental in him getting seriously *carried away*, she pushed herself away from him and said in mock reproof, 'Mr Warwick, you started all this!' Then they were laughing together and he kissed her briefly and told her he would desist, for the time being.

After dinner, they sat together in front of the fire and he asked her about her family.

'Well I was an only child,' she said slowly, 'and my parents—well, my father...' She stopped and sighed.

'Tell me about him, Davina.'

'He was such a difficult person.' She laid her head on his shoulder. 'He was intensely ambitious and he started and built up the business that was to be his downfall and it took a lot of drive and energy and expertise to do it. Yet looking back now I think he was rather insecure or something, because he was never really happy and he could be terribly critical, so that both my mother and I, we later discovered, always felt as if we were letting him down in some way or other. If I did well at school he always pointed out that it was possible to do better. If things went wrong at work, he took his frustrations out on her—oh, not physically, but she once told me she often thought that she was never a good enough mother or housekeeper or wife, yet she was all of those things. And he never let us forget that our growing wealth and so on was solely due to his efforts. This may seem crazy but we both acquired guilt-complexes, I think.'

'Which didn't help when it came to paying him back when the chips were down,' he said thoughtfully.

She swallowed. 'No. But I did it more for my mother than I did it for him, although she begged me not to. But I couldn't bear to see what she was going through.'

'Did you consciously decide on a course of passive resistance when you married Smith-Hastings?'

Davina thought for a while. Then she said bleakly, 'I was conscious of two things. That he frightened me in a way that was hard to define—perhaps I just didn't want to think about it too much; and that I didn't know how, without jeopardising my father's position, but *no one* was going to blackmail me into faking love. I told Darren that before I did it. He said it didn't matter.'

'How long were you together?'

'Twelve months.'

He moved abruptly. 'Twelve months of . . . coercion?'

'No . . . After about three months of, well, I suppose passive resistance on my part is a good way of putting it—his ego got in the way. I think he was genuinely stunned that he couldn't . . . bring me round. So he then set out to humiliate me, or so he hoped, with any willing woman he could find.' She smiled without humour. 'I was so relieved I just didn't care. But he made one stipulation. Either I put up a front or he pulled the plug on Dad. So I did. For nine more months I went everywhere I was commanded to, did all the kind of socialising he wanted me to, entertained all the people he needed me to, wore all the clothes his money paid for, got photographed and written about and even smiled at him in public and stood by his side like the dutiful wife I wasn't. He used to make a habit of parading his latest lover at all those parties and making sure I knew who she was.'

'My dear,' Steve took her hand, 'you deserve a medal.'

Davina grimaced. 'If Paul Grainger is to be believed, I didn't fool everyone.'

'He could have been talking from hindsight.'

'I suppose so.' She shivered.

'When did you find out he was going under?'

'My father was the first to tell me. He was . . . so shocked and ashamed—something Darren had relied on to keep him from telling me, incidentally—but apparently the rumours had been circulating for a while. It was when Darren started to want to transfer a lot of things into my name that I knew I had to get out. That he was a fraud as well as everything else. On the day my father died I did just that and left everything he'd ever given me behind.'

'He didn't try to stop you?'

'He did. He threatened me and all sorts of things. He said he had, after all, propped my father's business up—he didn't know my father had finally told me that there'd been a lot of promises and that for a while being associated with the Smith-Hastings name had kept the wolf from the door, just. But nothing had actually eventuated. But I went straight to a lawyer and set the thing in motion. And then I concentrated on keeping out of his way and trying to help my mother get over it all.'

'How is she now?'

'I don't think she ever will get over it but she wasn't left destitute, fortunately, though only by coincidence—she had a very elderly maiden aunt who died not long after Dad did and left her some money. She tried to give it all to me but I wouldn't take it and, well, she's finally got interested in of all things, saving endangered species like the rhino. She gets quite impassioned about it.'

'I'm glad,' he said quietly. 'But you're still left with this fear of Darren Smith-Hastings, even although it's been over for what... three years?'

'Yes, since the divorce came through. But I don't think I'll ever forget the last words he said to me—he said that if he ever got his hands on me again, I'd regret the day.'

She shivered again and he drew her closer and said drily, 'I'd like to get my hands on him but possibly they were only the words of a man who'd taken several severe joltings to his ego.'

'I keep telling myself that, but when you've been forced to do—certain things, it's not easy to believe it.'

'Do you feel safe now?'

'Oh, yes...' She stopped.

But all he said was, 'Good.' And he took her to bed presently.

It was a Lord Howe special the next day. Sunshine, a sparkling sea and a wide, clear blue sky.

Steve told her about his plans over breakfast. 'I'm going to take you to all my favourite spots. Bring your camera and your costume.'

She looked up eagerly but then her expression became a bit wary.

'What?' he queried.

'I...would hate to bump into Paul Grainger.'

'You won't, he left yesterday.'

'How do you know?'

He smiled slightly. 'I know a lot that goes on here. Any more objections?'

'Not one...'

It was a marvellous day and it gave her a new insight into Steve Warwick. She told him a bit about it as they sat on the thick, lush turf of the Clear Place looking out over Mutton Bird Island, Wolf Rock and Mount Lidgbird, and ate the picnic lunch she'd made.

'You really do love this island, don't you?' she said a bit dreamily as she thought back over all he'd shown her so far, the fantastic banyan trees and many others, the mutton bird holes, the Valley of Shadows, the spot on the cliff edge above Middle Beach where he'd pointed out two white terns flying in tandem, swooping and wheeling in perfect unison and as if they were flying just for the love of it.

'Yes, I do. I think it's in my blood.'

'How much time do you spend on the mainland?'

'Quite a lot.' He grimaced. 'I don't know if it was a conscious policy of my forebears but we acquired little bits of this and that, all quite humble at first but they've mushroomed now to the extent that I decided to go public in quite a few of them so there's not only myself and the family to consider but shareholders as well.'

'Darren—that was his forte, he always reckoned,' she said involuntarily. 'He saw himself as a corporate raider *par excellence*. But when interest rates went through the roof, he—well, he blamed the banks for being prepared to lend him so much.'

'It happened to a lot of them.'

'But basically you must enjoy such a diverse empire, mustn't you?' she said with a tinge of curiosity.

'I have to confess I do. I also look upon it as a trust, to keep it all going and healthy, wealthy and wise, and I enjoy the cut and thrust of commerce so I couldn't, much as I love it, simply live here and watch birds. But I couldn't ever envisage not being able to live here a lot of the time, either.'

'So you have the best of both worlds,' she said slowly.

'Perhaps.' He leant back on one elbow. 'The one thing I haven't done yet is provide any heirs to carry on the tradition. It's probably hard for outsiders to understand but I think most of us who have roots here regard the island as a bit of a sacred trust too. I think it comes from the isolation of the place as well as how self-supporting it's always been.'

'The Kentia palm,' she murmured. 'It is a bit amazing, isn't it? And still going on.'

'Yep! Although we only sell seedlings now, as opposed to seeds.'

Davina lay back and crossed her arms behind her head. 'It's so lovely,' she said softly, relishing the warmth of the sun and the clear air.

He looked down at her from close range so she could see the little yellow flecks in his eyes. 'So are you. I wonder if you have any idea of what I'd like to be doing right here and now?'

Her lips curved. 'I don't think it would be legal.'

'Not even an embrace?'

'Oh, well, perhaps.' But at that moment they heard voices approaching and they sat up, laughing quietly.

'So much for the isolation,' he said wryly. 'By the way, I'm taking you out to dinner tonight.'

'Thank you, but I can——'

'This will be educational as well as epicurean. You'll need to bring your camera.'

'Oh. Why?'

'Well, you know all those mutton bird holes in the ground we've seen?' She nodded. 'The adults,' he continued, 'leave their chicks in the holes all day while they fly out to sea to do a spot of fishing. They all return at more or less the same time just before dark and unerringly find the right hole in the ground. It's quite a sight and there's a restaurant ideally positioned above Ned's Beach to watch the spectacle while you have a pre-dinner drink.'

'Oh!'

'Mmm. In the meantime, I'm going to try and find you some Masked Boobies, unfortunately named birds one feels, but also well worth the sight.'

'Lay on, Macduff!'

*   *   *

But they didn't find any Masked Boobies and were laughing about that as they got back to the cottage, late in the afternoon.

'I'm tempted to think they didn't want to be found,' she told him. 'Perhaps they're embarrassed about their name?'

He grimaced. 'We'll see them tomorrow, anyway. I thought we might take Candice to Ball's Pyramid— they're always flying around the base of Mount Gower. Do you need to rest before we go out? We've done a hell of a lot of walking and climbing.'

'No,' she said, 'and a hell of a lot of that sort of gentle rambling we did today is small time to someone who has climbed Mount Lidghird! But I am going to soak in that bathtub for a little while.'

'Done,' he said. 'I've got a few calls to make.'

'I'm surprised there's a telephone.'

'The two things I insisted on were the shower and the phone.'

It was blissful in the tub with a haze of lavender-scented steam rising above her—she'd found the lavender oil in the credenza. And just as she was thinking reluctantly of getting out, Steve came in.

'I'm coming,' she said ruefully, and stood up.

'I wasn't coming to chase you up,' he replied and held out a hand to help her climb over the steep side of the tub. 'I was actually coming,' he went on, 'to feast my eyes on you. I've been plagued by visions of you without your clothes all day, you see.'

'I...' Davina stopped and felt herself starting to colour. 'Well, here I am,' she said a bit breathlessly, as his gaze wandered over her wet body, the sweep of her hips and thighs, the small mound of her stomach, her waist, her rosy, satiny breasts with their darker rose velvety tips. 'I can't help feeling a bit like a B-grade actress without her clothes, though,' she added involuntarily.

'Don't,' he said barely audibly and put his hands round her waist. 'I was not only wrong but a bloody idiot when I said that. You're exquisite—why, oh, why did I ever mention mutton birds?' And he looked into her eyes wryly.

'There's always later,' she said softly, and moved into his arms.

'Not if you do that,' he murmured.

'I'm only going to do it for a fleeting moment more. Steve——' She stopped and looked up at him.

'Say it, Davina.'

'I . . . thank you for a lovely day.' Which was not what she'd been going to say and she thought he might have guessed because something flickered briefly in his eyes, but she moved away and reached for a towel before he could comment. She also said brightly, 'Give me twenty minutes and I'll be ready.'

He paused and she held her breath but in the end he said, 'OK. I need a shower myself.'

She dressed with unsteady hands and the knowledge in her heart that she'd been almost unbearably tempted to say—I love you . . .

'I like that dress,' he said from the doorway.

She looked down at the chalk-blue dress she'd worn once before. 'Thanks. It's the kind of dress it's nice to be in.'

He pulled the towel he'd tied round his lean hips off casually and reached for his clothes. Davina turned away and started to brush her hair at the old-fashioned dressing-table. But, before she'd finished, he loomed up behind her in the mirror, still without his shirt and still with droplets of water on his broad shoulders and in the tawny, springy hair of his chest, and their eyes met in the glass. She was a little shocked to see the vulnerability in hers and blinked a couple of times then saw him smile absently as he looked down at her and slid his hands round her waist again as he said, 'Davina?'

'Yes...' she answered uncertainly.

'Don't go away from me.'

'I...I'm not.'

'Good.' He turned her to face him and fixed the collar of her dress that was a little awry and added, 'Are you sure?'

'Yes, I'm sure,' she whispered.

'Then shall we go and witness these blasted birds before it gets too dark?' He took her chin in his fingers and kissed her lips very gently.

'Oh, yes, please.'

And so it was that she arrived at the restaurant unable to help feeling reassured about some things, but still with the weight of what she'd nearly said on her mind—to be confronted by Mary Hargreaves, who greeted Steve delightedly and confided that she was on her own; she just hadn't felt like cooking after a tough day at the office, and how she'd so wanted to talk to Davina at the cocktail party but hadn't somehow got around to it...

CHAPTER EIGHT

AFTER the barest hesitation, Steve said, 'Well, you'd better join us, Mary.'

'Oh, no! I didn't mean that——'

But he said with a grin, 'Don't be silly. I'm sure Davina would like to meet you.'

'Of course,' Davina agreed with a smile, because there was really nothing else to do; the restaurant was small and she couldn't help feeling sorry for Mary Hargreaves, anyway, who had unwittingly given so much away the moment she'd laid eyes on Steve . . .

So they watched the mutton birds returning and Davina took some photos, then they sat down to eat. Davina discovered that Mary worked for the island board, that she was basically a bright, cheerful person, intelligent and cultured, probably in her late twenties, as well as being attractive and forthright. What she hoped in her heart was not so was that the four years Mary had spent away from the island had been spent changing herself into a more suitable person for Steve Warwick—perhaps not altogether consciously, but with it at the back of her mind. Because she couldn't help remembering what Steve himself had said about how Mary *had* changed.

She found that she was exerting herself so that it would be a pleasant meal, and saw Steve look at her strangely once, but pushed on regardless. Until Mary, who had rather carefully made no reference to Davina's position in the Warwick household, did say with a frown, 'You know, I'm sure I know your face, Davina.'

'That——' Davina stopped and bit her lip.

'That would be from when she was married to Darren Smith-Hastings,' Steve said, and as Mary's eyes widened with shock he went on, 'Would you like to come back to the cottage with us for a nightcap?'

'The... cottage?' Mary said uncertainly and Davina winced inwardly for her.

'Yes. We're eluding Lavinia and Loretta for a few days.'

'I—no, thanks, Steve, but I'll take a raincheck.' And, to her eternal credit Davina couldn't help thinking, Mary Hargreaves did battle with her emotions briefly—she swallowed visibly—and came up smiling. 'In fact, I think I'll leave you two alone right now! I've taken up enough of your time as it is. Thanks for a lovely evening—I'll get them to split the bill——'

'No, Mary.' Steve stood up as she did. 'This one's on me,' he said quietly.

'You're upset,' Steve said a while later when they were back in the cottage.

'I...' Davina stood in the middle of the lounge and twisted her hands. 'Yes.'

'Why?'

She closed her eyes. 'I can't help feeling sorry for her. I thought it was a little public and brutal to kill her dreams stone-dead like that.'

He came to stand in front of her and, as her lashes lifted, for a moment he was like the old Steve Warwick she'd first seen at the airport. Impatient, dangerous, big and worldly. He said evenly, 'My dear, I only wish I could have done something about Mary years ago. But how do you? I have never, I repeat, led her on.'

Davina sighed and shrugged. 'I don't know but...why did you tell her who I was, as well as making it so obvious we were...together? And I mean that from my point of view as well as hers.'

'Because we are together. Are we not?'

'Yes, but——'

'And because everyone will know it anyway and you can't change who you were.'

'But I've spent years——'

'I know, but while you're with me there's no need to hide.'

'How——' her throat closed but she made herself go on '—long will I be with you, though?'

He gazed down into her eyes. 'That's up to you, Davina. Do you want to—have it out now? I'm quite happy to. Do you want me to tell you that I'm falling in love with you? I am, so——'

'Steve,' she gasped.

He smiled a little grimly. 'What's so impossible about that?'

'I...well, how can you be sure?' she whispered.

'There are certain quite uncompromising signs. I can't help feeling you might have noticed them yourself, and in yourself,' he added with lethal gentleness and a pointed look down her figure.

'Steve, why are you angry?' she said barely audibly and with a tightening of her nerves.

'Am I? Could it be because I get the feeling you don't want to discuss this? You don't want it known we're sleeping together——'

'You're right,' she flashed suddenly, then frowned in exasperation. 'What I mean is I don't want it broadcast the way you did——'

'You mean, in other words, you'd rather pretend it's not happening?'

She took a breath. 'Of course not—I'd rather it was just between you and me,' she said flatly.

'Davina—it can't be, unfortunately. Not here.'

She bit her lip and looked up at him with shadowed, wary eyes.

'And what,' he said after about half a minute, 'is your reaction to the fact that I've fallen in love with you?'

She licked her lips. 'I have to tell you that this afternoon I nearly said the same thing to you, but——'

'So, what the hell are we arguing about?' he murmured and pulled her into his arms suddenly.

'Where it's going to lead, probably,' she whispered.

'If it's wedding-bells you want——'

'No!'

But he suddenly held her harder. 'Why not? OK, perhaps I could have phrased that more delicately, but what were you planning to do—come back and work out your month as both my housekeeper and my mistress? Stay here and hide yourself away until we proved it was only a passing attraction? Tell me, Davina?'

'You said...*you* said——' She stopped abruptly as a sense of fright and a new sense of anger took hold of her, as well as what she thought might be a grain of truth... Anger and fright because Steve in this masterful kind of mood made her feel vulnerable and made her remember her resolution never to allow another man to dominate her, even one who had brought her so much pleasure and delight. Truth, because it suddenly occurred to her that he had a dilemma on his hands. How *were* they going to go on? But what kind of a fool would she be to allow herself to be rushed into marriage like this when in her heart of hearts she still had some question marks?

'I know what I said.' All of a sudden his hands eased on her body. 'And I'm not reneging.' His lips twisted. 'Just rushing my fences. Why don't we remove this discussion to our bed? I feel I—say things with more fluency there.'

And she was helpless as he moved his hands on her through the thin material of her dress.

He insisted on undressing her himself this time. Nor did he say a word as he took her clothes off item by item, until she couldn't help smiling as she said, 'I thought this was supposed to be a discussion?'

He looked up with a wicked little light in his eyes but kept his hands cupping her breasts—there remained only one thing to dispense with, her panties. 'Perhaps that was a misnomer—a body poem might be a more appropriate term for this. Which I was hoping might speak for itself.' And, so saying, he laid her on the bed and drew the last wisp of lace and silk away, his fingers lingering on the soft skin of her inner thighs, and other places where the lamplight turned her skin to gold and rose.

And she lay naked and quiet beneath his hands for a while, then raised her hands and curled her fingers in the rough, springy hair of his chest. 'I have to say I love your body poems,' she said, but that was the last coherent thing she said for quite a while as he bent his head and began to tease her nipples with his tongue.

And later, when she was lying drowsily and dreamily in his arms, she thought he might have been right. Some things between them did speak for themselves, and always had. So why was she holding back? *Was* it too soon? Well, it was only a bare fortnight but... Did she honestly believe he was the kind of man who would marry her simply to get over the awkwardness of things? No, but... Well, this dot in the South Pacific with its small, interwoven community, not to mention his grandmother and his stepmother, was probably about as awkward a place to choose to have an affair as you could find, but... How to know if this emotion was going to last them a lifetime, how to know... It popped into her mind with a suddenness that caused her to stir briefly, then hold herself deliberately still so he wouldn't notice. But she couldn't hold her thoughts still... Such as— how to know whether she hadn't happened along when Steve Warwick was thinking about who he was going to hand his empire down to, was being beleaguered by his grandmother to the point of driving him round the bend, was uncomfortably conscious of being the object of another woman's dreams—in other words, needed a wife.

'What?' he said into her hair.

'I—what do you mean?' she whispered.

'You feel as if you've gone away from me again.'

Oh, God, she thought, he's so...he knows me so well; why don't I just put an end to this and say yes? But she said instead, 'I was thinking that your female relatives are being uncharacteristically—reticent.'

She felt him laugh soundlessly. 'That's because I threatened them with total banishment from Lord Howe if they were any other way. You know, I don't know what's worse, Lavinia and Loretta at loggerheads or in cahoots.'

Davina ran her fingers through his hair. 'I'm surprised that Loretta didn't know who I was,' she said, as that, too, just occurred to her.

'She does.'

Davina's fingers stilled. 'She told you?'

'No. She refused to tell me. She was also of the opinion that the least said about it, the better.'

'But——' Davina digested this slowly '—how did it even come up?'

'She was the first one to recognise Paul Grainger at the party. She came and told me it could be a problem for you—she'd noticed him staring at you, apparently. When I asked her why, she said, "I'll leave her to tell you that herself if she wants to, but, if she does, don't be shocked and if I were you I'd keep it to yourself." I didn't get a chance to tell her I already knew...most of it. She also said she felt as guilty as hell. I wasn't sure why but I guess—I could guess,' he said drily.

'For almost forcing me to go to the party and wearing that dress; I must have been mad,' Davina whispered. 'So...why did she think the least said about it the better?'

'You'd have to ask her that yourself, but I should imagine she thought you wouldn't want it broadcast about, which you've just told me you don't and of course I can understand it, but——' he paused '—it was obviously bound to come out sooner or later.'

'Yes,' Davina said very quietly, but wondered why she felt unsure, wondered what was niggling at the back of her mind but refusing to surface. She didn't get a chance to wonder long because the phone rang, splitting the night with its jarring jangle.

They both jumped and her heart started to pound as Steve sat up swearing. 'I told them——'

'Maybe it's not them,' she whispered. 'Why would they ring you up at about midnight?'

'You don't know Lavinia as well as I do,' he said grimly, but thrust the covers aside and padded out to the kitchen.

Davina pulled the sheet round her as she heard him answer and say, 'Hello? Lavinia, I warned you . . . what? OK. Yes, got it. I'm coming right now. Uh, Davina? I'll bring her back to you.' He put the phone down.

'What is it?' Davina asked anxiously as he came back in and started to pull his clothes on.

'Sydney Radio has picked up a mayday call from a yacht in this area. They're co-ordinating a search and want us to help.'

Her eyes widened. 'Help? How?'

'By plane; there's nearly a full moon. And by boat as soon as daylight comes.'

'What will you be doing?' she asked fearfully.

'I'll be going up in the plane—don't worry,' he said with a brief smile, 'I have an instrument rating for night-flying, and I won't be alone. Look——' he sat down on the bed '—this could take days. You'll be better back with them.'

'I didn't know you flew,' she said inconsequently.

He grimaced. 'There are probably a few other things you don't know about me, either. I've had a licence since I was twenty, but to get back to *you*——'

'Steve, I think I'd rather stay here.'

'No, Davina. It's not practical. For one thing you'd have to chop your own wood; just do as I say, there's a good girl.' He stood up and continued to dress.

Davina stared at him in the dim light of the kerosene lamp they hadn't doused, and realised with a tightening of her nerves that this was one of the times when to argue with Steve Warwick would be like knocking her head against a brick wall. That it would be quite useless to tell him that she felt totally unprepared to face his grandmother and Loretta, straight out of his bed. She did say tentatively, however, 'I could go in the morning.'

'That would only be putting off the evil moment. Look, I've got a few calls to make while you get ready and pack.'

It was surprisingly easy.

Both Loretta and Lavinia were up and looking anxious and they welcomed Davina quite naturally, even off-handedly as they gave Steve more details.

'Two adults, *three* children and a dog!' Lavinia said immediately. 'Sydney Radio says the transmission was very broken up, but apparently they're taking water, they're a bit confused about their exact position and they don't have an EPIRB.'

Steve swore beneath his breath. 'Where are they from?'

'New Zealand. On their way to Brisbane.'

'Right. I'm off.' He took a padded jacket from the hall stand and turned back to them briefly. 'Er—look after each other, girls. I'll check in whenever I can.' And he was gone.

It was Loretta who broke the sudden silence his departure caused. 'What on earth is an EPIRB?'

Lavinia came to life. 'It's some sort of an emergency radio beacon; it's quite small and portable so if you have to take to a lifeboat or a dinghy you can take it with you, and when it's activated it transmits on a frequency that can be picked up by aircraft or satellites in the area giving them its exact location—something like that and *no one* on an ocean-going voyage should be without one,' she said sternly. Then her expression softened. 'Let's have a cup of tea. It's so good to see you, my dear Davina. Are——?'

'Davina!' Candice came into the kitchen in her pyjamas looking like a little owl. 'You're back! I thought you'd forgotten me.'

'Not so, Candice,' Davina said with a warm smile. 'Steve and I were going to take you to Ball's Pyramid tomorrow but now—well, I'm sure there'll be other days.' As soon as she said it, she noticed Lavinia and Loretta exchange a look that she interpreted as being one of relief mingled with complacency, and she thought incredulously—of course, they didn't know what was going on but now they think it's...in the bag, so to speak. And she sighed inwardly.

She was up with the dawn the next morning and relieved to see it was a beautiful, clear day again.

So what do I do now, she thought, as she hugged her knees and pushed her hair off her face. Go back to being a housekeeper? Well, there's no harm in making breakfast, is there...?

Lavinia was the first to come downstairs but she went straight into the study and put a call through to the airport.

'He's still out,' she said briskly, coming into the kitchen. 'They've been back once to refuel but they've made no sightings.'

Davina poured her a cup of tea. 'Daylight will help, surely.'

Lavinia grimaced. 'It's a huge ocean out there. And if they've abandoned the yacht and are floating around in a tiny dinghy, well, it can be like looking for a needle in a haystack. Thank you, my dear. You're looking very well, I must say!'

Davina could think of nothing to reply other than, 'So are you, Mrs Warwick.'

'Do call me Lavinia,' Lavinia immediately responded. 'Everyone does—er——' she said delicately, but Davina was saved by Loretta who came in yawning and wearing the most marvellous housecoat, causing her mother-in-law to turn her attention to her. 'Loretta! I don't think I've ever seen you up this early.'

'I don't think I've ever been up this early,' Loretta said glumly. 'But I couldn't stop thinking about *three* kids and a dog.'

'Ah, well, Steven has been involved in a few of these searches, if anyone can find them, he can.'

To which Loretta replied, 'You're probably right. Is that bacon and eggs, Davina? Do you know, I think I might break my golden rule and have some if you've got enough.'

To which Lavinia then said a shade tartly, 'They're fattening.'

'And I'm well on the way—is that what you're trying to say, my dear Lavinia?'

Davina turned away and hid a grin. It was obvious some things would never change between these two, but it might give her a bit of breathing space, she reflected.

Fortunately, too, in some respects although not others, it was one of Maeve's days and she greeted Davina like a long-lost friend. 'Glory be! Am I glad to see you, Davina! Now I'm not sure what you're back as, I mean to say, well, never mind, shouldn't have opened my mouth, but the last time I was here, the day after the party when you weren't, do you think Mrs W. didn't give me a hard time? She had me washing windows and walls. Not that she didn't get stuck in herself, I will give her that but that's not the easiest thing to live with either! Er...you in charge here again?'

'I...think so, Maeve.' Davina was only too conscious of the embarrassment in her voice, so she forced herself to sound more positive. 'Would you like to start with the ironing this morning?'

Maeve's wide beam was all the answer she needed.

But, indeed, Lavinia took herself off to the airfield just after Maeve's arrival and stayed there.

'Glory be!' Loretta echoed Maeve's sentiments, coming upon Davina as she sat on the terrace with a cup of coffee and watched Lavinia drive away. 'You're not still playing housekeeper, by any chance?' she enquired.

Davina looked at her ruefully over the top of her mug. 'I don't quite know what else to do.'

'So...it hasn't resolved itself?' Loretta said carefully, sitting down herself. 'Do you mind me being a sticky-beak?' she added with her own brand of forthrightness that, in Loretta, was hard to resist.

Davina thought for a bit, staring down at her cup then she lifted her eyes to Loretta. 'Steve told me you know who I was.'

'Yes. I twigged pretty early—when you said you'd worn my clothes, in fact. Not that I meet everyone who buys them, but I like to keep track of who wears them.'

'Why did you tell Steve the least said about it the better?'

'Darling,' Loretta said slowly, then gestured. 'Well, for one thing, I didn't think you'd want it bandied about——' She stopped.

'But there's more, isn't there?' Davina said quietly, with that little niggle at the back of her mind surfacing again.

Loretta sighed. 'Your ex has been pretty active lately. I happened to see him on Paul Grainger's show which was why I nearly died when the bloke showed up here. He . . . the bastard was incredibly clever,' she said coldly. 'He contrived to make you out as a scheming little bitch who'd walked out on him in his hour of need and he also didn't stop there. I've seen two magazine interviews along the same lines.'

Davina breathed deeply. 'And you thought Steve would be shocked and wonder about me?' she said, in an even quieter voice.

Loretta shrugged. 'Men can be . . . let's face it, I'm sure it's only human for men to side instinctively with men and women with women, but no, I'm not accusing Steve of that, although I certainly copped enough flak from him about his father, but then I did take his mother's place. But the real thing was, I didn't want *you* copping any flak. People talk here—people talk everywhere, but here . . . well, I was afraid that because it's such a small community you might find people looking at you strangely and I thought, heaven knows, what's between you and Steve seems to be complicated enough without that, yet.'

'So it could always be a complication?' Davina suggested.

Loretta said strongly, 'Not to those who matter, Davina. And if you think that's just easy wisdom, believe me, I know what I'm talking about.'

Davina put her cup down and wrapped her arms around herself. 'Thank you for believing in me, by the way, but I'm not sure why you do.'

'Ah, well, I happened to meet him once, your ex. Very attractive et cetera but he struck me as being incredibly full of himself. He also,' she said gently, 'tried to make a pass at me while you two were still married. If Steve knows all about it, though,' she looked at Davina queryingly before she went on, 'you must know if he believes you.'

'He does. He...does.'

'So, what's the problem?'

'Me,' Davina said barely audibly. 'He's asked me to marry him but I don't know if it's too soon, I don't know if it's just one of those intense physical attractions that will fade, if he's decided he *needs* a wife—I have all these doubts. I'm racked by them,' she said and wiped away a foolish tear. 'You see, I swore I would never be forced or rushed into anything again, but what's almost worse is I've got the feeling that if I ever saw Steve Warwick fall out of love with me, I think I'd die. Although I sometimes also think he's a hard man to love; he's so determined and——'

'Arrogant—one of those masterful types, not to mention downright bloody-minded sometimes,' Loretta supplied. 'And too much of a sheer male to know he's rushing things,' she added with an exasperated look.

'Well, it is a bit difficult,' Davina said awkwardly.

Loretta smiled. 'At least you've got Lavinia on your side.'

'If she ever sees Darren doing his bit, she might have second thoughts. Not——'

'No, it really is none of her business,' Loretta said ruefully. 'Not that that's ever stopped her. Well, pet, I think you're just going to have to take a stand. If you don't want to be rushed, dig your heels in—not that *that* will be easy; there's an awful lot of Lavinia in Steve, but I guess I don't have to tell you that.'

Davina smiled briefly.

Steve came home for a short while that evening, for a meal, a bath and a few hours' sleep. Davina cooked the meal and they all ate together and discussed the search, so once again there was little embarrassment. For one thing, it was too sobering to think of five people and a dog adrift in a dinghy.

But before he took himself to bed, he came into the kitchen and took her into his arms with no regard for whoever might wander in.

'I'm sorry about this,' he said, rubbing his chin on her hair, 'but I'm out on my feet.'

She looked up into his eyes and touched an unsteady finger to the blue shadows on his jaw, unsteady because she was suddenly weak with love. 'Don't be. It's not your fault.'

'How are they treating you?'

'Just fine,' she said wryly. 'I took Candice for a swim this afternoon and they actually both came with us. And I took some interesting, I hope, photos of the three Warwick ladies, together.'

He grimaced then his eyes narrowed on her in a way that made her pulses start to hammer. 'I don't suppose you'd like to come and...soothe me to sleep?'

'No.' Her lips curved into a smile. 'What you need is pure sleep, Mr Warwick.'

'Pure sleep?' He lifted an eyebrow.

'You know what I mean,' she said ruefully.

'Do you mean—put us in a bed together and I might not get much sleep?' he suggested gravely.

'That's exactly what I mean,' she replied equally gravely.

He laughed and kissed her. 'You'd be quite right.' Then he sobered and sighed. 'You've no idea how frustrating it is to know they must be out there somewhere...' He shrugged.

'So there's been no more radio contact?'

'No. Which makes it seem highly likely they've had to take to a dinghy or——' He stopped.

'Go to bed,' she said softly. 'Things will look better when you're not so tired.'

But the next day and night yielded nothing and most people began to believe the yacht had sunk with no survivors, although the search continued.

It was on the third morning of the search that Lavinia picked up the post and brought home two letters for Davina—one from her mother and one in a type-addressed envelope. She put her mother's in her pocket and opened the other one with a faint frown, only to go white and feel dizzy as she read it.

My dear Davina, so that's where you're hiding? I don't suppose I need to tell you how I found this out; he really is a little germ, isn't he, although quite useful? But the big news is, by a happy coincidence, I've fought my way out of all my financial difficulties and paid back all my debts. I won't bore you with the details, but I found someone to go into silent partnership with, who believed I was the unlucky victim of the recession, fiscal policies and so forth, which I was, and because my ideas made him a lot of money, quite a lot of it has now come my way and I'm respectable and wealthy again. What, you may be wondering, has this to do with you? I'll tell you. I'm now in the position of not having to stand by and watch you marry another man. Thanks to Paul, I know a lot about Steve Warwick and his quiet but substantial empire, I know all his companies that are public with him as chief shareholder and, on the day you accept his ring, I would begin to attempt to shoot down every one of them, like sitting ducks. Would I succeed? I like to think so, and even make myself some more money in the process, but if I don't, I'll still have a hell of a lot of fun along the way while causing *him* merry hell. You see, my dear, there are some things I can never forgive or forget. And you shouldn't forget what a genius I was at takeovers in my heyday...

Davina let the letter flutter to the kitchen floor then stooped to pick it up hastily as Candice came in.

'Davina—are you OK?'

She swallowed and tried to pin a smile to her lips. 'Fine. Did you want something?'

'You don't look too good, but I just came to talk to you,' Candice confided. 'Mum's going through a stage of trying to be a better mum, probably just in case I get spirited on to a yacht and drowned and then she'll have to feel guilty all her life.'

Davina couldn't help but laugh and then found herself saying curiously, 'Is she such a bad mum?'

'Well, what she was trying to tell me was that she might not be a con...' Candice paused and looked to Davina for help.

'Conventional?'

'That's it, a con-ven-tion-al mum, but she does love me. Do you think you'd be one of those?'

Davina looked at her affectionately 'I don't think you can know until you become a mum. But there are worse things than having an unconventional one; I think that all that matters is that she really loves you. And so does Lavinia, and so does Steve, and, while they may sometimes argue about you, it's because you're such a special person to them.'

'Like you are to Steve?' Candice looked at her enquiringly.

Davina returned that clear, innocent gaze and wondered how on earth to answer. But all she could come up with was, 'Perhaps.' And knew it sounded lame but Steve himself walked in at that moment.

And the way he said, 'Hi, ladies!' made them both look at him searchingly.

'Have you found something?' Davina asked.

'Just as we landed, a report came in from another plane that they'd made a sighting. Not quite sure what it is, there's a lot of low cloud cover in the area, but at least it's something. I've just come to grab a cup of tea and take some sandwiches back.'

'Right.' Davina shoved Darren's letter into her pocket and turned towards the counter. 'Candice, you can help me, you can butter the bread—why don't you have a quick shower?' she added over her shoulder.

'Will do,' he said, paused, his gaze on her, then he smiled briefly and walked out.

He came back in ten minutes and drank his tea thirstily. By this time Lavinia and Loretta had been apprised of the news and were discussing the possibilities eagerly, but Steve stayed only minutes then took Davina by the hand and said, 'Come outside with me for a minute.'

She went reluctantly and as soon as they were out of sight and earshot, he said, still holding her hand, 'What's wrong?'

'Nothing,' she said quickly, perhaps too quickly, because he frowned immediately.

She tried again. 'I think we're all a bit uptight. I know I've never been involved in a sea search this closely and it—gets to you.'

'Sure?'

'Yes, Steve,' she said quietly. 'Look, don't even think about me; you need all your energy to concentrate on finding them.'

'It's very hard not to think about you,' he said with a slight smile at the back of his eyes. And as her hand trembled in his, he lifted it to his lips and kissed her knuckles. 'I'm off.'

She watched him drive away, then went to her chalet and locked herself in.

*　*　*

It was only after she'd reread Darren's letter a couple of times that she remembered her mother's and was horrified to discover that her mother had read the magazine articles Loretta had mentioned and was distraught and disturbed. 'I don't know why he's doing it,' she wrote, 'but the way he's telling it makes him come out smelling of roses and you, well, like some cheap girl who only married him for his money.'

'Which I did,' Davina murmured with irony, and looked unseeingly at the wall. And she thought of that old saying about women scorned with a bitter little smile.

Then she sighed and forced herself to think about Steve and the whole situation she now found herself in. Of being in the position to bring possible ruin to a man she loved. Was it as simple as that? she wondered. And discovered that a lot of things had become curiously simple, such as finally admitting to herself that she loved Steve Warwick far too much to do that to him.

Sounds so dramatic, she thought, and noble! Only I don't feel noble; I feel frightened, helpless, exposed as if I've been hung up on a line like dirty washing—will Steve think of me that way one day? Could a relationship survive that kind of strain? He did say to me once that I should never have done it, married Darren... And I know Darren too well to disregard his threats. But there is one thing I can do... and the sooner I do it, the better.

But it was a good few minutes before she stirred, and made a phone call. Then she started to pack. And when that was done she looked around and swallowed, hating herself a little for leaving as she was hoping to be able to, like a thief in the night, and decided to write a brief note which she would leave in the Land Rover at the airport. Nor did she feel any better when she was able to get her bags into the Land Rover and drive away unseen. But, at the airport, things changed...

'I'm sorry, Mrs Hastings,' the girl behind the counter said nervously, 'but we've discovered we've overbooked the flight.'

Davina frowned and opened her mouth but the girl rushed on, 'What with so many aircraft being diverted for the search it's been...we've had to cancel quite a few flights, although they've found them!' she said, brightening. 'All alive and fairly well.'

'That's wonderful news,' Davina said with relief but added, 'Are you sure there's no room for me?' She looked out at the plane waiting on the apron and bearing the distinctive emblem of Steve's airline, which she'd hoped to be able to avoid but the urge to be gone had overcome that—then around the little terminal where there appeared to be only two other passengers waiting just five minutes before take-off.

'Well.' The girl cleared her throat, then brightened. 'There are only a few passenger seats on it. The rest is freight.'

'But you must have known that when I rang,' Davina pointed out, suddenly feeling a cold, sinking sensation.

The girl looked confused, miserable, then blurted out, 'The thing is, Mr Warwick left strict instructions that we weren't to fly you out in any circumstances, only I didn't know it when I took your call—Sam,' she called over her shoulder, 'could you come out, please? I think I need help.'

Sam turned out to be the airport manager and he looked both sheepish and harassed.

'Is this true?' Davina demanded coldly.

''Fraid so, Mrs Hastings.'

'But you don't even work for him! There's absolutely nothing you can do to stop me going on another flight on another airline—he doesn't own the airport!'

'That's what I told him,' Sam said eagerly but his face fell. 'There is no other flight today, though. We put on a couple of extras this morning to clear the backlog but— that's it. Incidentally,' he added, as a plane zoomed into view down the strip, 'that's Mr Warwick, he's just landed. So you can have it out with him.'

Davina closed her eyes, feeling about as trapped as she'd ever felt. Where to run? Where to hide? On Lord Howe? Nowhere...

''Then will you tell him that I'm waiting for him in the Land Rover—as I've no doubt you'll tell him everything else,' she said sardonically and swung away on her heel.

Mount Gower and Lidgbird had never been more beautiful, with some lazy cloud touching their peaks as she looked at them from the place she'd first photographed them.

Steve had come out of the terminal with his face grim and set and simply climbed into the Land Rover, slammed the door and driven them off. Not home, she'd prayed and indeed, he'd turned off the road and driven across the grass to the point above Lovers' Bay, as she now knew it was called.

'OK,' he said through his teeth, as the engine died. 'Want to go first? I presume you're going to tell me all the stupid, cowardly reasons you've come up with as a bar to us being right for each other.'

Davina took a breath and tried to control the anger that rushed through her but it was useless. 'No,' she said tautly, 'but I'm going to ask you this—how *dare* you do that to me?'

'Because I know you too well, Davina. You're still wearing your crown of thorns and loving it—do you think I couldn't see it? God knows what triggered it today but something as sure as hell did. I can only assume you've been moralising on things, such as...' He held up a hand and ticked off his fingers, and it was the most curiously insulting gesture she'd seen for a time. 'It's too soon, it's too awkward because of Lavinia, Loretta, Candice, Mary, probably, and the devil alone knows who else you have in mind. It's too...physical?' He glanced at her with so much irony in his eyes she flinched, and he went on with searing mockery. 'Too hot to last—is that what you think, Davina? You're going to have to go a long way before you find a man who will fall in love with you without wanting to sleep with you, my dear, and possibly even a longer way before you find a man *you* want to sleep with as much as you like to do it with me.'

She gasped and went white before she could speak, he said, 'Sound a bit crude to you? Believe me, it's true, and I think you should know better than most what a crucial thing it is in a marriage. You didn't exactly practise passive resistance with me. You didn't, for example, seem to mind it when I——'

'Stop,' she whispered, still white to her lips. 'If you expect me to believe a marriage to you could last when you can say things like those you've just said to me, you're mad!'

'Not mad, just a realist,' he said quite gently. 'You want me to tell you we'll love each other madly until the day we die? Well, there's no way I can prove it and you can't either and we could prolong this argument for six months and still be unable to prove it. But to run away because it's a possibility we mightn't? Well, you know what I think that is.'

'Yes. And I have to tell you I'm happy to be a stupid coward, Steve, and I'm going to *go*.' She stared at him, her mouth set, her eyes angry and determined. 'I told you once before about the aversion I have to any man dominating me the way you're attempting to, and whether I have that aversion rightly or wrongly is not the point. The point is I can't stand it and again, whether I like to go to bed with you or not doesn't change that. But the most important point of all is that, when you know a marriage is unlikely to last even six months because of it, you'd be crazy to even contemplate it.'

'All right,' he said abruptly and switched on the engine. 'You've got it.' He drove the Land Rover round in an arc towards the road, so fast that she clutched the door.

'Where?' she said furiously. 'Would you mind telling me that?'

'Wherever the hell you want to go. The plane I just landed in is going back to the mainland, and you can go with it. Actually, Pete is the pilot. Remember Pete? Now, doesn't that add quite a twist to our little saga, Davina?'

She could have hit him, but there was worse to come.

At the airport he was coldly businesslike as he arranged for Davina's departure, and he totally ignored everyone's unspoken embarrassment. Then he stood back and said with a dry smile and quite audibly to all in earshot, 'You were an excellent housekeeper, Davina. It's a pity we didn't just confine ourselves to that, isn't it? Remember me when you're lying alone in bed at night.'

She stared into his eyes disbelievingly, then turned away and walked out on to the tarmac.

CHAPTER NINE

IT WAS with the greatest effort of will that Davina presented a normal image to her mother when she arrived at the flat they shared in Sydney that evening.

'Davina! Darling, I didn't expect you home yet. Has something gone wrong? Not my letter——'

'No.' She kissed her mother and looked round the familiar flat with a sigh of relief. 'No, it was just one of those impossible jobs. I . . . walked out.'

Her mother grimaced. 'It must have been bad for you to do that; you're usually so competent, and not only at housekeeping but handling these people—but you know, I do wish you'd think of doing something else. It's . . . not much of a life. What did you think of the island, by the way? Plenty to photograph?'

'Oh, it's a paradise in that respect,' she said with the barest tremor. 'Do you know, Mum, I've got the feeling that that will be my last job as a temporary housekeeper? I don't quite know how, but I'm going to concentrate on photography for a while. I've saved a bit in the last few years so—who knows, you might be looking at another Cecil Beaton. In the meantime, there must be jobs as—fashion photographers et cetera.'

'I'll help you look,' her mother said eagerly. Then she sobered. 'About Darren——'

'Don't worry about him, he can't hurt me now,' Davina said, and turned away.

Her mother hesitated but didn't persist.

But that night when Davina went to bed, she closed her door and stared around at her room and at all the photos pinned to the wall, and wondered if she had the simple will to gather together a portfolio and try to hawk her wares around the picture libraries and agencies. Whether she had the energy to seek commissions or jobs as a staff photographer, whether she could turn her flair to something like fashion, whether she was only ever destined to be a passionate amateur...whether she didn't feel like dying.

She sat on her bed and dropped her face into her hands. And discovered that no amount of telling herself that Steve Warwick was impossible to the point of being hateful at times, could do something as essentially dictatorial as what he'd done, had been brutally frank enough to make her doubt he could truly fall in love with anyone, no amount of it quite stilled the small murmur within that she was both stupid and a coward. Nor could it conquer the numb, barren feeling that was creeping up in her. And she wondered how her anger could drain away like this...

It was the next night that the memories attacked her. Lying alone in bed, she remembered his last words and was flooded with cameos of the times they'd been together, such as the morning after the night at the cottage when she'd told him about her father and Darren...

She'd wakened first, seen that he was still sleeping deeply and eased herself out of bed without waking him. She'd pulled on a T-shirt and shorts and slipped out to breathe in the clear, rain-washed air, the smell of damp earth, and to trail her feet through the sun-spangled grass. Then she'd decided to take him breakfast in bed, but there'd been no wood chopped fine enough to light the stove and she'd regarded the axe and the chopping block outside the back door, and thought, It's probably quite simple to chop wood; why don't I try to add it to my list of accomplishments? I'm sure Lavinia would approve, if no one else... It hadn't proved simple at all, and Steve had appeared at the back door only wearing a brief pair of underpants.

'I was going to bring you breakfast in bed,' she'd explained ruefully, and explained about the wood.

A lazy smile had lit his eyes and he'd rubbed the stubble on his jaw as he'd said, 'It's quite simple really. Let me show you how.'

She'd laughed. 'That's what I thought, but...' She'd gestured ruefully at the mess she'd created.

So he'd picked up the axe and, within a few minutes, reduced several sturdy blocks to fine, even slivers. But as he'd put it down, she'd remained transfixed by the sheer perfection of his body, the long lines of his back and the flow of muscles of his shoulders, the ease and strength of his movements, the compact hips and the springy darkening hair that ran down to his loins... And she'd stood rooted to the spot and blushed hotly like a silly, dizzy schoolgirl. But the growing wry query in his eyes had suddenly gone oddly gentle and he'd taken her hand and taken her inside, saying only, 'It's OK. You do it to me all the time.'

'I feel a bit foolish...'

'Don't.' He'd tilted her chin and looked into her eyes. And then he'd taken her back to bed and their love-making had been piercingly sweet...

Was I mad? she wondered, coming back to the present and her lonely, torment-filled bed. When will I get over this raw, wounded feeling?

But over the next few days it grew so much that she doubted she would ever recover from putting Steve Warwick out of her life, however much cause she might have had to do it. But not only did the pain grow, it seemed to pose these questions—had she walked out on a man not because he could be difficult and arrogant— he could also be wonderful—but because she was still terrified to trust herself to any man? Why had she not defended herself by telling him about Darren's letter— because even in her anger at the time, she'd perceived it would only be putting a totally unfair burden on him? Or because she *was* a coward and it had been something to hide behind in her mind?

I don't know, she thought. Perhaps I will never know unless I can put Darren behind me forever...

Her hands stilled suddenly. She was in the small third bedroom they'd converted to a dark room, developing her Lord Howe photos, and she was only putting herself through the pain of doing that because her mother was dying to see them and very determinedly helping her to put together a portfolio. Not that it was one of Steve in the dish emerging in the solution, but the house, with Lidgbird and Gower in the background, and as she stared down at it, then closed her eyes as it evoked memories of him that took her breath away, it made her wonder, with sudden tears streaming down her cheek, how you could love and hate a man at the same time. Was the hate bit mainly because you were afraid to love, though? she asked herself. Was it because *he* couldn't break down that barrier that he was so impossible and—the rest? But, of course, there was still Darren . . .

She opened her eyes suddenly and started to breathe erratically. Could she do it? The one thing that might free her of him forever? If she did do it, could she go back to Steve Warwick and say—you make me hate you sometimes but mostly I love you, so if you still want to take a chance on me, I'm prepared to take that chance, too?

A week later she landed once again on the tiny strip at Lord Howe and had to beg a lift from the airport.

The lovely house browsed in the afternoon sunlight, a wood-hen scuttled into the grass beside the barbecue and there was not a soul in sight. There was also not a soul at home as she hesitated at the front door then let herself in. Upstairs, the three bedrooms Lavinia, Loretta and Candice had used were bare, but there was evidence in the kitchen of a meal recently consumed and so she went into the den and sat down to wait.

It was an hour before he came and the sun was starting to sink. She heard the Land Rover and tensed, then she heard him come in through the kitchen and took a frightened breath and found she couldn't move. She'd left her bags outside the den door, though, and she heard him start to walk towards the stairs then stop and change direction and, with her heart beating like a train, she looked up as he loomed in the doorway. And they just stared at each other wordlessly for a long moment.

Until her nerves or whatever got the better of her and she stood up abruptly and said jerkily, 'I hope you don't mind me doing this, letting myself in I mean. I . . .' She stopped and swallowed.

'Of course not,' he said quietly and seemed about to say more but stopped, too.

'Steve.' She twisted her hands. 'I've come to tell you something. Will you let me just say it? I don't know if it will explain anything to you but I need to try.'

'Yes. Why don't you sit down again?'

She did and he came to sit opposite her and it struck her that he looked tired and tense with lines beside his mouth. But she tore her mind away from those kind of things deliberately, and from the fact that he'd given her no clue as to how he felt about her walking back into his life like this. It doesn't matter, she told herself, it's myself I'm squaring... 'Steve...oh, would you read this first?' She drew Darren's now crumpled letter from the pocket of her jeans and handed it across to him.

He frowned down at it and started to read, then he lifted his eyes to hers and said in that same quiet way, 'Go on.'

Oh, God, she thought, I've left it too late... 'That,' she said with an effort, 'came the day I left. It was the reason, or so I thought, for going like that. It wasn't until later that it occurred to me I could do something about it, and that unless I did it I would never know...how things really stood for me and...between us.'

She paused then said, 'So I took steps to ensure that Darren would never be any threat to you again. I went to see him and I took with me a prepared statement that detailed most of our life together. It included the pressure he and my father had brought to bear, it included how he, Darren, had tried to offload assets into my name and a couple of other highly unethical methods he'd employed that I'd unwittingly become aware of—and it included the name of every women he'd ever flaunted before me and every night he'd spent away from home.'

'And you had proof,' Steve said, not as a question, she was to realise later, but as a statement.

'Yes, I had proof. I kept a diary. Not with anything like this in mind; it just seemed to ease the pressure a little to have *something* to confide in. He... at first he didn't believe me, he didn't believe I would do it—go on Paul Grainger's show and tell all. Then he tried to bluster that no one would be interested anyway, but when I pointed out that a few of those names belonged to women married to some very prominent men, he changed his tune. He had the gall to tell me I was about as low as anyone could go but, well, to cut a long, unpleasant story short, we did a deal. In return for my silence, he will stay out of my life now, forever.'

'Davina——'

'No, let me finish. I'd always thought I would feel dirty if I was ever forced to do anything like that, that the mud would have to cling somehow, but I found that it didn't. And it had something to do with this... I may have been a victim once but I was in danger, as you pointed out to me a couple of times, of becoming a willing victim. And not only because I was still letting him frighten me and still living under the shadow of what he did, but because I was afraid to ever try again with anyone else. I'm——' she looked down at her hands then up into his eyes '—not that any more.'

She thought he sighed, and thought she knew why with an arrow of pain going through her heart as she said, 'But if, with the benefit of hindsight—or whatever, you... you——' her voice shook '—don't still want me, I'll go——'

'No, you won't,' he said with something of his former arrogance. 'Not ever again——'

'Steve,' she whispered, her eyes widening, but she got no further because he stood up and pulled her up into his arms and held her so that she could barely breathe.

'You didn't have to do that; you didn't have to put yourself through all that just because I was such a bloody fool,' he said torturedly as he kissed her hair and her eyelids. 'I could have killed him; I nearly did when I found out.'

'You knew?' She stared up at him out of stunned eyes.

He picked her up and sat down with her. 'I went to see him a couple of days after you did. Loretta, for reasons best known to herself, finally told me about the magazine articles and gave me a more in-depth idea of the Paul Grainger interview. Well, to be honest,' he said, 'after I all but drove you away, I took myself off for over a week and they couldn't get hold of me. I . . .' he laid his head back '. . . don't remember ever feeling more manic or . . . unable to believe what was happening to me. That I couldn't have the only woman I'd ever really loved and nine-tenths of it was my own fault. But, when I got back, Loretta collared me and told me a few home truths, and between us and Candice and Lavinia, we worked out that you'd got a letter that had upset you that day. I thought that the two people who were most likely to have upset you were either Darren Smith-Hastings or Paul Grainger. So I started with Smith-Hastings.'

Davina stirred, but he ran his fingers down the side of her face very gently. 'I was a bit amazed at his reaction—well, first of all he flatly refused to see me so I had to . . . employ certain methods; I did a bit of ranting and raving to his secretary until she let me in. Then he looked as wary as hell and the first thing he said was, "It's over, Warwick, you can have her. We've done a deal."' He stroked the side of her neck. 'I asked him to elucidate. He said, "I'm sure she's told you all the dirty details herself." I said I'd like to hear them from him; nevertheless. I think,' he said slowly, 'he realised when he'd finished how close I came to throttling the life out of him. I don't think he'll ever forget it.'

Davina moved her cheek against his shirt and closed her eyes at the wonder of the feel of his fingers on her skin.

'So, now you're wondering, I would imagine, why I didn't come straight to you?'

'No,' she murmured. 'I mean . . .'

He kissed the top of her head. 'It was all Loretta's fault. She told me I'd been rushing you and probably frightening the life out of you myself. I knew something I'd been doing hadn't been working. So, I thought, once again, perhaps I can wait, perhaps I should wait—that you wouldn't have done what you'd done unless . . . So I came home, but these last few days have been pure hell. I can't sleep, I can't settle to anything; I *know* I wouldn't have lasted much longer.'

'Steve,' she said softly, and put her hand to his face, 'I love you——'

But he said imperatively, 'Hang on. There's more. You see, I knew it all myself, I didn't really need Loretta,' he said drily, 'to spell it all out for me. I knew that after a ghastly experience like that, you were hurt and humiliated and afraid of men. What I couldn't do——' his voice dropped '—was give you the time you needed. Oh, I tried a couple of times, only to find I couldn't wait; I'd never wanted a woman so much, I'd never lived with the fear that I mightn't be able to have her, not only to hold, but to *love* in all senses of the word—and it drove me in a way I'd never known, even for me. But I did try to hold off, in a sense. I said and did some things all designed not to pressure you. And to hide from you,' he said grimly, 'the fact that what had happened to me *was* a bit like being hit on the head, and that every day it was becoming clearer to me that I couldn't let you go; that I was exactly the kind of man you thought you feared most, who would want to dictate to you and . . . well, I suppose you know what I mean.'

'Steve——'

He kissed her and said, 'Let me tell you all, my darling; I don't want there to be any misunderstandings between us again. One of my stratagems,' he said, with a sudden weary little smile, 'was not to let you think I was trying to *push* you into marriage. I thought I could do that better by showing you how inevitable it had to be. You said to me once that you'd thought it would be high drama when we slept together, if we ever did—I tried to make it something that was warm and tender and fun and something you could see lasting us a lifetime. I tried,' he said very quietly, 'despite the fact that wanting you was the most intense thing that had ever happened to me, to play it down, to. . .' He shook his head.

'You did—you made love to me so wonderfully it . . . made me forget everything else that had ever happened to me.'

'But it didn't make you *believe*—and the way you were sometimes led me to think I never could make you believe. That's what drove me the day you left, drove me to do the things I did and say the things I did. I knew something had gone wrong and I knew I should have been there with you, but...well, when exactly what I feared might happen apparently had happened, I lost my head and reverted true to type, I guess. I also knew I only had one shot left, the one I was deathly afraid of playing and it was this—if you do ever marry me, Davina, I'll *never* let you go. But that's the problem: that's not only the kind of man I am but the way you affect me. I probably don't have to tell you that; you may have worked it out for yourself. I'm the one kind of man you told me so often you could never——'

'Steve.' And this time her voice was low and husky but insistent. 'Let me tell you what I've worked out. I've worked out that I'll have a terrible life with you.' But a smile curved her lips as he tensed and she went on softly, 'I know you'll go to any lengths to get your own way, but you see, there's not a lot you'll have to fight me about now. I think we're in some agreement about the basics such as—the fact that I can't live without you. I'm lost and lonely, there's this awful ache within me that only you can stop; I *believe* now, Steve, and it was *me* I was fighting more than anything and there was only one way I could resolve it, which I've done now...'

He stopped her right there, and as he kissed her and held her she felt his heart beating against her breasts in a wild, exalted way that matched her own.

'A lot of people will still tell you you're mad,' he said some time later as she lay flushed and breathless in his arms, thoroughly kissed and still held as if he was afraid to let her go.

She slid her fingers through his tawny hair and down to those lines beside his mouth. 'Some people have told me the opposite.'

He raised a wry eyebrow. 'I can't imagine who, if you discount Lavinia—she's not altogether unbiased.'

'Well, let's see. There's Maeve. She told me the day we first met that you were a lovely man——' her lips trembled '—a bit hard to handle maybe, but really, no wife could ask for more. In the way of washing and ironing machines.'

He laughed and said wryly, 'My one fan.'

'No. There's Candice. She even stood up for you one day when Lavinia and Loretta were—commenting on how difficult you could be.'

He grimaced. 'I can imagine. Candice will be thrilled by this turn of events, by the way.'

'I'm glad. I felt terrible about walking out on them, too.'

'I wouldn't,' he said with a wicked little smile. 'You achieved more harmony between Loretta and Lavinia by getting them to gang up on me than I would have believed possible. They're still ganged up, incidentally.'

'Loretta also told me to…well, think twice about you.'

'Loretta,' he said a shade drily, 'will be impossibly smug now.'

'But she also told me that you were an…all-or-nothing man, one of those masterful types, perhaps, but…' She smiled into his eyes.

'Now, that,' he said slowly, 'I have to agree with, the all-or-nothing bit.' He stopped, then went on in a deep, quiet voice, 'I had these fantasies. Of you, with no shadows in your eyes, in this house, in the sunlight with me, the rain, whatever… I thought of kids: a girl who looked like you and could twist me round her little finger as well as trust me to always have her best interests at heart; a boy I could pass on to not only everything I love about this island but the love and respect I had for his mother. I couldn't get them out of my mind.'

'Oh, Steve,' she whispered with sudden tears in her eyes and buried her face against him.

'No more tears?' he said later, as they lay side by side in his bed, loosely entwined.

'None.'

'You're so beautiful.' He traced the outline of her body from her waist to her hip and thigh.

'And you do things to me—I probably don't have to tell you about.'

'You could show me.'

'OK.' And she freed herself, but only briefly. 'There, how's that?'

He moved beneath her weight and slid his hands down her back to the curve of her bottom, and looked into her eyes with just a suggestion of the old wicked glint she knew so well. 'You have me entirely at your mercy,' he also said softly. 'If I moved, I'd be... lost.'

She pressed her breasts against his chest and wrapped her arms around him. 'Don't move. I'd be lost, too, you see. What I'm really trying to tell you is how much I love you.'

'Ah. But, if we... got lost together, would that not be an affirmation of *our* love?'

She laughed down at him, and he caught his breath. 'What?' she queried, sobering.

'They're gone,' he said with an effort. 'The shadows in your eyes are—gone.'

She relaxed. 'Because you made them go—Steve?'

'Yes?'

'I don't think I can last much longer...'

'I'm so glad,' he said with an intensity in his voice and his arms, 'because *I* was going to try to tell you how much I love you, but now I'm going to have to show you.'

And he did.

'Now what do we do?'

It was over a year later and the occasion was a christening party. Lavinia was in blue silk and wearing her pearls. Loretta was wearing little, but what there was of it was a vivid yellow watermark-taffeta creation, and she glowed with good health and good humour. Candice was pretty in pink and absorbed with the baby as was Davina's mother, and Davina herself wore a distinctive shade of chalk-blue.

There had been a few wrangles. Lavinia had been unable to prevent herself from commenting on how highly unsuitable Loretta's dress was for a christening, as well as delivering herself of a lengthy discourse on childcare to anyone who would listen. Loretta had retaliated by stating with a lazy smile that if this baby's mother had to put up with all she'd had to put up with, she might as well prepare herself to acquire the patience of a saint.

But it was none of this that caused Davina to look up from her three-month-old baby into Steve's eyes as she asked that question with love and laughter in her own. Because this was no violet-eyed, fair daughter they'd had baptised Caroline Warwick. This little girl had little hair but what there was of it was definitely gingery, and not at all unlike her father's. She also had grey eyes that were developing little yellow flecks in them and, moreover, was given to announcing her likes and dis-

likes in a way that reminded them all of one person—
her father.

'Now what do we do?' he repeated with a wry little
smile and putting his arm around her. 'Keep trying?' he
suggested, looking into her eyes with a mixture of devilry
and love that still made her heart beat rapidly. 'I seem
to be somewhat addicted to it, as you may have noticed,'
he added.

'As it happens, so am I, Mr Warwick,' she replied
gravely, and lifted her face for his kiss.